Heroes in Training
4-Books-in-1!

HEROES IN TRAINING

Heroes in Training 4-Books-in-1!

Joan Holub and
Suzanne Williams

Aladdin

New York London Toronto Sydney New Delhi

ALADDIN

An imprint of Simon & Schuster Children's Publishing Division
1230 Avenue of the Americas, New York, New York 10020
This Aladdin hardcover edition June 2015
Zeus and the Thunderbolt of Doom text copyright © 2012 by Joan Holub and Suzanne Williams
Zeus and the Thunderbolt of Doom illustrations copyright © 2012 by Craig Phillips
Poseidon and the Sea of Fury text copyright © 2012 by Joan Holub and Suzanne Williams
Poseidon and the Sea of Fury illustrations copyright © 2012 by Craig Phillips
Hades and the Helm of Darkness text copyright © 2013 by Joan Holub and Suzanne Williams
Hades and the Helm of Darkness illustrations copyright © 2013 by Craig Phillips
Hyperion and the Great Balls of Fire text copyright © 2013 by Joan Holub and Suzanne Williams
Hyperion and the Great Balls of Fire illustrations copyright © 2013 by Craig Phillips
Cover illustration copyright © 2012 by Craig Phillips
Also available in individual Aladdin hardcover and paperback editions.
All rights reserved, including the right of reproduction in whole or in part in any form.
ALADDIN is a trademark of Simon & Schuster, Inc.,
and related logo is a registered trademark of Simon & Schuster, Inc.
For information about special discounts for bulk purchases, please contact Simon & Schuster
Special Sales at 1-866-506-1949 or business@simonandschuster.com.
The Simon & Schuster Speakers Bureau can bring authors to your live event.
For more information or to book an event contact the Simon & Schuster Speakers Bureau
at 1-866-248-3049 or visit our website at www.simonspeakers.com.
Designed by Karin Paprocki
The text of this book was set in Adobe Garamond Pro.
Manufactured in the United States of America 0217 FFG
2 4 6 8 10 9 7 5 3
Library of Congress Control Number 2015938514
ISBN 978-1-4814-6019-4 (hc)
ISBN 978-1-4424-5264-0 (*Zeus and the Thunderbolt of Doom* eBook)
ISBN 978-1-4424-5266-4 (*Poseidon and the Sea of Fury* eBook)
ISBN 978-1-4424-5268-8 (*Hades and the Helm of Darkness* eBook)
ISBN 978-1-4424-5270-1 (*Hyperion and the Great Balls of Fire* eBook)
These titles were previously published individually by Aladdin.

⚡ Contents ⚡

Zeus and the Thunderbolt of Doom

For our editor goddess, Alyson Heller
—J. H. and S. W.

Greetings,
Mortal Readers,

I am Pythia, the Oracle of Delphi, in Greece. I have the power to see the future. Hear my prophecy:

Ahead I see dancers lurking. Wait—make that *danger* lurking. (The future can be blurry, especially when my eyeglasses are foggy.)

Anyhoo, beware! Titan giants now rule all of Earth's domains—oceans, mountains, forests, and the depths of the Underwear. Oops—make that *Underworld*. Led by King Cronus, they are out to destroy us all!

Yet I foresee hope. A band of rightful rulers called Olympians will arise. Though their size and youth are no match for the Titans, they will be giant in heart, mind, and spirit. They await their leader—a very special, yet clueless godboy. One who is destined to become king of the gods and ruler of the heavens.

If he is brave enough.

For saving the world will not be greasy. Um—*easy*.

Prologue

Over the teeth and past the gums, look out, belly, here Zeus comes!" King Cronus, the big bad king of the Titan giants, tossed up the object he held. It flew high above his head. As it arced downward, he caught it in his mouth. Then he swallowed. *GULP!*

Far below, five Olympian childgods were being held captive deep inside his dark, giant belly. They heard squishy sounds. Something

came whooshing down the Titan king's throat like a snowball rolling down Mount Olympus. They all pressed back to avoid being squished by whatever was coming.

Splat! The new arrival hit the bottom of Cronus's stomach.

"Hello?" Poseidon whispered into the darkness. "Are you one of us? Another Olympian?"

No answer.

"Maybe he's dead," Hades said in a gloomy voice.

Just then Cronus burped big. As his mouth opened, light speared down his throat into his belly. The young childgods gasped.

"That's no Olympian. It's a stone!" Demeter exclaimed.

Hera ran her hand over the smooth cone-shaped stone. It was half as tall as she was. "This thing could be our ticket out of here!" she whispered in excitement. Feeling around, she found a sharp fish bone left over from Cronus's supper last night. She began to blindly scratch a message on the stone: *Help us! We are in Cronus.*

"Wait a sec," Hades said when she told them what she'd written. "I'm not sure I want to leave. I mean, Cronus swallowed us as babies, and we haven't been outside since. Who knows what dangers might be lurking out there? Besides, I like it in here." For whatever reason, gloomy, smelly places didn't bother him.

"Then stay if you want to," said Hestia. "But the rest of us want *out*!"

Poseidon nodded. "Yeah. Do you want to be trapped in here forever? If we don't get out, we'll never age past ten. Cronus's magic spell won't let us."

Before Hades could answer, they heard Cronus bark out an order to his army. He was riding into battle in the town of Delphi. Soon they heard the clank of swords all around them. There were more shouts—and screams, too.

The Olympians quickly made a slingshot out of an old Minotaur wishbone and a strip of elastic sinew. (There was all kinds of gross stuff lying around in Cronus's belly.) After they set the inscribed stone into the slingshot, they pulled it back tight.

On the count of three, they let it go. *Boing!* The cone-shaped stone shot up Cronus's throat and burst out of his mouth. The fact that it knocked out one of his front teeth as it exited was just icing on the cake.

Although they had no way of knowing it, the stone hit the ground rolling. It skittered and bumped its way down a hillside. Then it came to rest at the bottom of a set of marble steps that led up to a temple.

Immediately a white-robed woman wearing eyeglasses hurried down the steps to pick it up. It was almost as if she'd been expecting the stone to arrive! Hugging it to her chest, she disappeared into the temple with it.

CHAPTER ONE

Ten Years Later

*F*lash! Lightning zigzagged down from the sky.

Crack! It struck a hundred-year-old oak tree and split it in half. A tremendous clap of thunder boomed overhead.

"Yikes!" shouted ten-year-old Zeus. He dropped the wooden sword he'd been practicing with. Leaping out of the way of the falling tree trunk, he took off running. He had a feeling the next bolt would be aimed at him. Why? Because he'd been struck by lightning dozens of times already in his short life.

A wild wind whipped through his dark hair as he raced for safety. With his heart beating faster than a hummingbird's wings, Zeus dove through the entrance of a cave. A new lightning bolt struck the dirt just outside it, barely missing his foot.

Flash! Boom! The storm raged all around him as he cowered behind a boulder. This cave was his home—the only one he'd ever known. And as far back as he can remember, thunderstorms had been a daily event here in Crete.

He was terrified of them. Who wanted to be hit by lightning after all? It tossed you into the air and rattled your brain. He ought to know!

But that wasn't the scariest part. Each time he'd been struck, he'd heard a voice murmuring to him, *"You are the one."* What could it mean?

Another flash of lightning sliced through the clouds, followed by rumbling thunder. Rain lashed the ground. It flattened the grasses in front of the cave and churned the dirt to mud. But then, as suddenly as it had begun, the thunderstorm moved off. Clouds lifted, the sun came out, and the earth began to dry again.

Feeling braver now, Zeus stuck his thumbs in his ears and wiggled his fingers. "Nyah, nyah, you missed me," he taunted toward the sound of distant thunder.

Nearby he heard the clanking sound of a bell followed by a bleat. *Maa!* A goat trotted into view. "Amalthea!" He threw his arms around the goat's neck, glad to see her unharmed.

Moments later a nymph slipped free of a slender willow tree and scampered over to milk the goat. When she finished, she wordlessly handed Zeus a rich, creamy cup of milk. He drank it down in a single gulp, then nodded to her in thanks.

Stomp! Stomp! Stomp! The ground beneath them began to shake. It sounded like a whole army was heading their way. The nymph's eyes went wide.

"Hide!" Zeus hissed. He fled to the cave again while she leaped into the willow. Merging with its trunk and branches, she went invisible. Peeking out from behind the boulder, Zeus was relieved to see that Amalthea was nowhere in sight. He hoped she would stay away until this new danger passed.

Before long, three men marched into the clearing. Half-giants, by the look of them. They were so tall that their heads were even with the top of the nymph's willow. Yet they weren't as tall as a true Titan giant. True giants stood as tall as oaks!

These half-giants wore polished helmets and carried spears. Two letters were carved on their iron helmets and armor: *KC.* Which stood for "King Cronus." Which meant they were Cronies—soldiers working for the Titan king.

Zeus shuddered. Cronies terrorized the countryside, stealing money and food from farmers and villagers. Anyone who resisted was dragged off to a dungeon—or worse. He cringed lower in his hiding place.

One of the half-giants, a Crony with a double chin, scratched his big round belly. He gazed down the mountainside. "Lots of apple orchards down there," he said. "Should be easy pickings."

A black-bearded Crony laughed. "Especially since we can force the farmers to do the picking *for* us!"

Zeus trembled with anger. Half of him was ready to tell those half-giants off. But the other half was too chicken. Besides, what could he do? He was only a kid. They'd crush him like a bug under their humongous sandals!

He'd heard tales of others who'd tried to fight and had failed. Now everyone pretty much bowed down to the Cronies. It beat getting stomped.

Maa! Maa! Suddenly he heard the faint ringing of Amalthea's bell again. Oh no! She was coming back.

As the clinking grew louder, the Cronies spotted her. "Mmm. I fancy goat meat for supper," the double-chinned one said. He drew back his spear. Zeus opened his mouth to yell, *Stop!* But before he could, the half-giant dropped his weapon.

"Yeowch!" Double Chin yelped, slapping the back of his neck. Meanwhile, Amalthea trotted downhill again, out of reach.

The other two Cronies frowned at him. "What's with you?" Blackbeard asked.

"I got stung by a bee!" Double Chin grumped.

Zeus grinned as he watched the bee buzz around the half-giant's head and then fly off. It was Melissa.

Ever since he'd mysteriously arrived at the cave as an orphaned baby ten years ago, she had kept watch over him along with the nymph and Amalthea. He was glad for their companionship. Still, he did often wonder who his parents were and why they'd abandoned him.

The third half-giant, who sported a huge tattoo of a lion on his shoulder, looked around nervously. "We should go," he said. "In case there are more bees."

Zeus almost laughed aloud to think of King Cronus's fearsome soldiers being afraid of something as small as a bee. Normally Melissa wouldn't even hurt a fly. But cruel half-giants deserved whatever she could dish out.

"What's that?" Double Chin asked, staring toward the cave. Zeus shivered. Had he been spotted? If so, he was doomed! But then he realized what the Crony was really staring at— Zeus's drinking cup. He'd left it on the ground in full view!

Lion Tattoo was first to reach the cup. Picking it up, he sniffed it curiously. Then he held it upside down over the palm of one hand. "Fresh milk," he grunted as a few white drops trickled out. "Someone's here."

All three Cronies looked toward the entrance to the cave. Ducking his head, Zeus tucked himself small. If only he could merge into the boulder like the nymph had merged with the tree.

Footsteps pounded closer. Hot breath. Suddenly Zeus was plucked from his hiding place like a weed from a garden. His legs dangled helplessly in the air and his arms spun.

Holding him by two fat fingers, Double Chin stared at him, eye-to-eye, licking his chops. Zeus squeezed his eyes shut, as if doing so might make the half-giants disappear. Didn't work. And it didn't drown out the terrible sound of Double Chin's next words either.

"Fee, fi, fo, fun. I smell boy. Gonna eat me one!"

CHAPTER TWO

Good-bye, Crete!

P lease don't eat me! I'm pretty sure I taste picky. Like . . . like cave scum or bat poop," Zeus croaked out. "And I'm bony. I might get stuck in your throat."

Double Chin laughed. "Ha! Grease you up with a little garlic oil and I could swallow you whole, easy as pie!"

"Yum, pie." Blackbeard sighed longingly, like he was remembering pies he'd enjoyed in the past.

"Or we could take you to King Cronus and *he* could swallow you whole!" Lion Tattoo said. He winked at his pals. "The boy would have plenty of company down in the king's belly."

What's that supposed to mean? Zeus wondered. He thought about trying to wrench himself free from Double Chin's grasp. But the ground was a long way down.

"How should we fix him?" Double Chin asked the other two. "Grilled?"

"I vote mashed," said Blackbeard.

"Later," said Lion Tattoo. "Lunch will have to wait. We need to hit the road."

He must be the leader of the three, thought Zeus.

Double Chin set Zeus on the ground. Then he quickly whipped off his KC helmet. Bending down, he took it in both hands and stuffed it over Zeus's head. It was so big that it slid all the way down over his shoulders to his wrists.

Stunned, Zeus stared out between the bars of the grill in the front of the iron helmet. He was trapped in helmet jail!

He couldn't move his arms at all. The helmet was so tight, it pinned them to his sides. He tried running away but tripped and couldn't get up again. He rolled around on the ground like a bug on its back, unable to right himself.

Double Chin and Blackbeard shook with laughter. But Lion Tattoo roared, "Move it!"

Instantly Double Chin set Zeus on his feet again. Then he poked the helmet with the tip of his spear. "You heard him. Move it!"

Zeus moved it. What else could he do?

As they started down the hillside, something swooped down at them. The nymph had flown out of the willow. She was trying to save him! But the half-giants brushed her aside as if she weighed less than a leaf.

They'd gone only a few more steps when Amalthea appeared. The goat charged after them. When she caught up to Blackbeard, she leaped up and butted his behind.

"Why, you—" he yelled. Whirling around, he grabbed the goat around the neck.

"No!" Zeus gasped, sure that Amalthea was a goner. Suddenly he heard a buzzing sound above him. *Melissa!* She made a beeline for the half-giants.

Zeus cheered. "You go, bee!"

"Get away!" screeched Lion Tattoo, waving his hands in the air to fight her off.

Double Chin reached out and backhanded the bee hard enough to send her tumbling into a bed of daisies. Zeus was relieved to see Melissa crawl under a toadstool, unharmed.

Meanwhile, the wriggling goat slipped from Blackbeard's big hands and ran off. Blackbeard took a few steps after her. But when she zig-zagged to the top of a cliff, he gave up.

"Guess that goat got your goat, huh?" Zeus teased him. "Guess I'm too much trouble to keep around. Maybe you should let me go."

Blackbeard just glared at him.

"Not a chance," said Lion Tattoo, starting off again. "Little snacks like you eventually grow up into fighting men. Who knows what trouble you could cause us then?"

"Who? Me?" Zeus tried not to trip over his feet as he hurried to keep up with the giants. He was a ten-year-old boy. An orphan who lived in a cave. Although he liked to pretend to sword fight, he had no real skills. His parents, whoever they were, hadn't stuck around to teach him any. And though he longed to see the world, he'd never traveled anywhere. What possible trouble could he cause? He was a nobody!

Zeus forced out a giggle as he stumbled along. "Oh, ha-ha, hee-hee," he said. "I get it. You were joking, right? 'Cause there's no way you could be scared of me. That would be like being afraid of something as tiny as—" Cocking his head to one side, he pretended to think for a second. Then, brightening up, he glanced at Lion Tattoo through the grill: "—as tiny as a *bee*!"

The other two Cronies snickered. Lion Tattoo scowled. "As soon as we find some garlic oil, you are toast!" he told Zeus.

Blackbeard's stomach growled, and he eyed Zeus longingly. "Yum—toast."

Uh-oh! He'd better not act *too* annoying, Zeus decided. Because his captors might decide to eat him right now!

"Don't listen to them. I like you, kid," Double Chin said. "You've got spunk."

Zeus wasn't sure what "spunk" was. But he

hoped it wasn't something half-giants found tasty. "Does that mean you'll let me go?"

"Naw." Double Chin shook his head. "You're coming with us. We could use a little entertainment."

"Yeah, let's see how fast he can run," Lion Tattoo said with a sinister smile. With that, the half-giants went crashing down the mountainside. Because they'd made him march ahead of them, Zeus had to scramble to keep from being trampled. Tripping, he fell onto his side and rolled downhill.

Thunk! He came to a stop when he crashed into a tree trunk in the apple orchard. Luckily, the helmet protected him from harm. As he dizzily rose to his feet and staggered on, the three Cronies entered the orchard too.

They began uprooting trees with their bare hands. Stripping the apples from the branches as if they were grapes on a vine, they tossed them into their mouths. They stomped downhill, chomping and crunching. Whenever Zeus slowed, they prodded him with their spears to make him keep up.

At last they reached the sea. Zeus hadn't seen a single person the whole way downhill. Everyone must've heard the Cronies coming. They weren't exactly quiet. And having heard them, anyone with an ounce of smarts would be hiding.

"Look!" bellowed Double Chin, pointing to a ship tied up to a dock. "Free transport."

The ship's sails were half unfurled as if its crew had quickly abandoned ship. The Cronies tossed Zeus on board, jumped in, and set sail.

"Wait!" Zeus yelled. "Where are we going?"

CHAPTER THREE

Trouble Ahoy!

Never you mind where we're headed, Snackboy!" Lion Tattoo growled in answer to Zeus's question.

Maybe he was still feeling touchy about everyone laughing at his fear of bees. Still, knowing that this half-giant leader was afraid of something so small made Zeus feel less embarrassed about his own fear of thunderstorms.

"We're heading for the Mediterranean Sea.

Going all the way to Delphi," Double Chin told him.

"Delphi, *Greece*?" Zeus asked, astonished.

"No—Delphi on the moon," joked Blackbeard. "Of course Delphi, Greece. Gonna join up with Cronus's army there. And it'll be a long, *hungry* trip," he added pointedly.

Argh! That didn't sound good. Still, Zeus couldn't help feeling a little excited. His cave in Crete had been so boring. (Except for the thunderstorms!) He was grateful to the nymph, bee, and goat for taking good care of him there. But deep down, he'd always believed he was destined for a life that was more awesome.

For years he'd thought his parents would come back to get him one day. But over time that dream had faded. Now that he was off to see the world, maybe he'd find *them*. If he didn't become snack food first!

"What are you going to do in Greece?" he asked.

Blackbeard grinned evilly, patting his belly. "Bake us some boy pie, first thing."

Zeus thought it best not to reply to that. As the half-giants guided the ship, he watched it cut through the sparkling blue waters of the Mediterranean Sea. He'd always longed for adventure. This would have been a fine one if he'd been with different, less hungry companions.

Seeming to sense his fear, Double Chin tried to reassure him. "Aw, just ignore him, Snack. We're all full of apples for now. Don't worry. You got hours to live."

He was nicer than the other two, Zeus decided. Sort of.

Suddenly the wind began to whip up. "Storm's on the way," Lion Tattoo noted, eyeing the darkening sky.

He was right, Zeus realized as he stared at the swirling black clouds overhead. This morning's thunderstorm was coming back. And now there was nowhere to run! Stuck in the middle of the sea, he'd be an easy target for the lightning bolts that seem to chase him wherever he went.

He tried not to panic. But as he heard thunder growl in the distance, he wondered how these half-giants might like him fried. By lightning.

The soldiers got busy adjusting the sails. The billowing wind filled them, pushing the ship along at a fast clip. Zeus stared out between the bars of his helmet jail, his eyes wild.

"See that storm? It's after me," he told the half-giants. "And if lightning strikes this ship, I won't be the only one to fry." When his captors didn't reply, Zeus hopped up and down. "Are you listening, you Cronies? You should sail back to Crete and let me go!"

Blackbeard reached out and whacked the side of Zeus's helmet. "Don't call us that! We hate that nickname. We're half-giants, got it?"

"Well, my name's not Snack either!" Zeus yelled, feeling grumpy himself. "It's Zeus."

At that, Lion Tattoo's head whipped around to stare at him. "Zeus? Hmm. Why does that name ring a bell?"

Zeus shrugged. When he'd been abandoned as a baby, the nymph had found him lying in a basket with a scroll tucked beside him. One word had been written on it: *Zeus*. That was all. No way this half-giant could possibly have heard of him.

"Incoming!" Double Chin shouted, drawing everyone's attention. He was pointing at the sky again.

In the faraway clouds Zeus saw five dark blobs soaring toward them. Whatever they were, the half-giants seemed worried about them.

Barely a second later the storm was upon them, lashing them with rain and wind. Waves rocked them to and fro, tossing the ship around like a toy. His three captors had all they could do to control the ship.

Thunder rumbled, closer now. "Here we go again," Zeus muttered.

But for some reason the lightning didn't strike him. And instead of trying to sink them, the wind was pushing them in the direction they wanted to go. At this speedy rate they would reach Delphi in no time. It was almost as if the storm wanted to hurry them along.

Caw! Caw! Zeus looked upward again. Those five black blobs had gained on them. They were birds! Big ones.

"Aghhh!" The half-giants scurried around in frantic circles on deck, darting alarmed looks at them.

"Some soldiers you are—scared of crows!" Zeus shouted over the wind.

"Those are Harpies, you idiot!" Double Chin yelled back. "They'll peck your eyes out in two seconds."

Zeus stuck his nose through the bars of his helmet jail and stared harder at the birds overhead. Whoa! They were bigger than he was, he realized. And they had long curly hair that blew out behind them as they dipped and rose on currents of air. Birds with *hair*?

Then he noticed something even weirder. They had women's faces! But what had him *really* shaking in his sandals was the sight of their curved, razor-sharp beaks. That, and the demented look in their beady eyes. He shuddered.

Quickly he gathered his courage. Those lady birds might be vicious, but they were also a distraction. And while the Cronies' attention was on them, he might just be able to hide. But where?

CHAPTER FOUR

Harpies

Trying to keep his balance on the bobbing ship, Zeus walked the deck searching for a hiding place. Any hiding place.

Just then the ship rolled hard to one side. He stumbled and tripped over the railing. Then he was falling. Tumbling overboard!

Splash! He hit the stormy sea headfirst, plunging deep. When he bobbed upright again, he coughed and sucked air back into his lungs. Stunned, Zeus watched the ship sail away.

He treaded water, kicking his legs hard. He didn't want to drown out here!

But with his shoulders trapped inside Double Chin's helmet, he had no chance of saving himself. The iron helmet was heavy. Sure, he could swim, but not without the use of his arms. Especially not in these wild seas. And he was pretty far from land.

"Help!" he yelled toward the ship.

To his surprise, it turned around and came toward him, tacking back and forth into the wind. Lion Tattoo was at the helm, looking oddly determined to rescue him. Why were they coming back? Were those apples wearing off? Were they hungry again?

When the ship got closer, Lion Tattoo pointed a finger at Zeus. "You! I just remembered where

I heard your name." He leaned over the side, trying to snag Zeus's helmet's grill with the hook on the end of his long harpoon.

Zeus frowned and backpedaled his legs. How could the half-giant have heard of him?

If Lion Tattoo really did know something about him, maybe he knew who his parents were. Zeus had been unable to learn anything about them over the years. But now hope rose in him again that he might discover something.

Just as the harpoon's hook drew near, a shadow fell over him. *Caw! Caw!* Zeus looked up. The Harpies!

Whoosh! One of them dove straight at him. Her dagger-sharp claws wrapped tight around the helmet's grill. Zeus ducked his head as far back inside the helmet as he could.

At the same time, Lion Tattoo swung his harpoon wildly. But all he caught was dead air.

Because Zeus was already in the clutches of the boy-pecking Harpies!

Up and up he went. Higher and higher. Then he was flying. Where were the Harpies taking him? Probably to their nest, where he would become Harpy bird-baby food. It seemed like all anyone wanted to do today was eat him!

Zeus wiggled around, trying to escape from the helmet. It began to loosen. He gave a hard bounce. Then he was free!

And falling!

Before he dropped far, claws wrapped around each of his arms and held him fast. Two other Harpies had grabbed him, one on either side. At least he was out of helmet jail now, though this wasn't much better.

"Where are you taking me?" he demanded. But his words were whipped away by the wind.

And so they flew onward, the ship swiftly becoming a mere speck in the distance.

He hadn't wanted to be the half-giants' snack. But he didn't want to be pecked to death by these bird-women or their babies either. All of a sudden, getting swallowed whole by Blackbeard seemed like the lesser of two evils.

Turning his head, Zeus stared at the far horizon. He could no longer see the ship or his home on the island of Crete. Was he never to see his friends again—the nymph, bee, and goat, who'd raised him for ten years? He'd wanted to see the world, but not *this* way! For now he was at the mercy of these crazy birds. And he could only wait and see what they would do.

Caw! Caw!

Heading north for Greece, the Harpies flew like the wind, staying just ahead of the storm. The firebirds formed a V shape, with one bird in the lead and two behind on either side. Every so often they changed places, as the lead lady bird tired.

Hoo-loob! Hoo-loob! Zeus turned his head and saw that a pigeon was now flying alongside them. A rolled-up piece of papyrus was clamped in its beak. A message! He could read only two words of it: *Capture Zeus.*

Huh? Zeus blinked his eyes a few times. Was his vision playing tricks on him? Maybe the high altitude was affecting his brain, causing him to see things that couldn't possibly be.

Less than an hour later the Harpies reached the shore of Greece. Far below them the harbor was full of ships. The pigeon dove, heading for one of them. They were military ships, Zeus realized. With dozens of half-giants on board.

He watched the pigeon deliver its message to a half-giant in a captain's uniform. After quickly scanning it, the captain pointed up at the Harpies. He shouted orders to his crew.

To Zeus's amazement, everyone began running around. They were giving chase. But there was no way these Cronies could catch them. They were on the ground. He and the Harpies were flying.

Why was the army after him, anyway? Were they hungry too, like the half-giants he'd met before? Surely there were other boys they could eat. Boys who'd be easier to catch!

The Harpies flew on, past hillsides covered with grapevines and olive trees. Now and then, Zeus saw a battalion of the king's Cronies marching in formation in the countryside. *Why so many?* he wondered. It almost looked like they were preparing for war!

CHAPTER FIVE

Bolt

I t wasn't long before Zeus spied a city below. Marble buildings with tall, white Ionic columns and smaller stone houses clung to a hillside. His winged captors dipped lower, going in for a landing.

Zeus's sandals touched down. He hit the ground running. Then he tripped and rolled in a series of head-over-heels somersaults.

When he finally came to a stop, he sat up

on the dirt road, feeling dizzy. The five Harpies stood in a ring around him. He didn't see any nests nearby. Or any hungry baby birds. *Good.* But what did these Harpies want?

The biggest of them stared at him and licked her pointy beak lips. The others had black eyes, but this one's eyes were red. She leaned in close and flapped her wings excitedly. *"Flea!"* she squawked.

Eew. Zeus pinched his nose between two fingers. Her breath reeked, and not in a good way. It smelled sort of like skunk mixed with stinky cheese. But where did she get off calling him a flea? Come on, he wasn't *that* small!

"Bick off, buds," he commanded. Not understanding him, the Harpies only cocked their heads curiously.

Zeus let go of his nose just long enough to repeat himself. "Back off, birds!" But they didn't back off, so he pinched his nose closed again.

Now all five birds began squawking at him. *"Flea! Flea!"* Bird breath surrounded him. Mega-stink!

"I'm not a flea! I'm a boy!" Zeus protested. Hearing the sound of footsteps and horses' hooves, he got to his feet. He peeked over the red-eyed Harpy's wing.

Beyond her a bunch of half-giants were swarming toward them! The birds' breathtakingly bad breath could probably knock them out at twenty paces. But whose side were these birds on? His or the half-giants'?

"Flea!" The red-eyed Harpy flapped her wings now as if shooing him away.

Zeus unpinched his nose again. "Oh, I get it! You mean *flee*? As in run? Good idea." He looked around. Behind him were steps leading up to some kind of temple. In front of him were smelly Harpies. And just beyond them were boy-eating half-giants.

He was no idiot, despite what the half-giants back on the ship had thought. "Thanks for the ride!" he told the birds. "Maybe I can do you a favor sometime." Seeing no better choice, he turned and dashed up the steps, taking them two at a time.

The Harpies lifted off, beating the half-giant attackers with their wings to delay them. Once he was inside the temple, Zeus looked for a way out the back.

The temple was round, but it wasn't very big. Its floor and walls were made of gleaming white marble stone. Tall columns stood all along its surrounding walls, and its roof was a dome. But there was no exit door.

Outside he heard shouts. Some of the Cronies

had managed to slip past the birds. Any minute now he'd be captured. He had to do something—and fast!

Zeus spied some small urns by one wall. But they weren't big enough for him to hide in. There was a low table standing right in the center of the floor. It was draped with a long dark blue tablecloth. And for some reason there was a big rock sitting on top of it. The rock was shaped like a cone and was about half as tall as he was.

Zeus dashed toward the table. He was hoping there was room enough for him to dive under it and hide.

Stomp! Stomp! Stomp! Too late! The soldiers were inside the temple now, almost upon him. Footsteps pounded closer. "There he is!" boomed a voice. "Get him!" called another.

Desperately, Zeus looked around for a weapon

to hold them off. Something. Anything! Seeing a long, jagged stick stuck point-first in the cone-shaped stone, he reached for it.

And pulled.

The jagged stick slid from the stone like a knife from a ripe peach. He'd been expecting it to be harder to get out. Now he stumbled backward under the force of his pull.

The bright white stick glowed in his hand. Its edges looked razor sharp, its blade highly polished. Only, it wasn't a stick at all, he realized. It was more like a sword. But not like any sword he'd every seen or heard about.

Swords were straight, not crooked like a zig-zag. And this thing was as long as he was tall. Yet it was lighter than the wooden sword he'd made back home.

Gripping it in both hands, he waved it at his attackers. It made a crackling, whooshing sound

with his every swing. He'd felt brave as he practiced with his homemade wooden sword earlier that morning. But this was a real fight. And now his hands shook.

The point of the zigzag sword struck the lead soldier's breastplate armor. Sparks flew. The half-giants stopped in their tracks.

Suddenly they were backing away, whispering in awe. "He pulled it out!" "Who is he?" "How could a mortal boy manage what no one else could do?"

Zeus stared in horror at what he held. Because he'd just noticed something really weird and kind of scary. The zigzag blade he'd pulled from the stone wasn't a stick. And it wasn't a sword, either.

No—instead, it was an actual, sparking, sizzling, terrifying *thunderbolt*!

CHAPTER SIX

The Woman in the Mist

W ait till King Cronus hears about this!" shouted one of the Cronies. He ran from the temple and clomped down the front stairs. Then he leaped onto his horse and galloped away.

The remaining half-giant soldiers continued to back away from Zeus and his thunderbolt. Seeing how scared they all were, Zeus felt braver.

"Yeah, that's right," he taunted. "You *better*

run!" He lunged, brandishing the bolt like he'd practiced with his wooden sword back home.

Cowering, the half-giants fled from the temple and down the steps. But they didn't go any farther. So how was he going to escape with them waiting outside?

One thing was for sure: He was not going to take this thunderbolt with him when he got his chance to run. He glanced at it out of the corner of one eye, worried. What if it decided to turn on him, jumping out of his hand to strike him?

Bending low, he carefully laid it on the marble floor. Then he let go of it. Or tried to, anyway.

His fingers wouldn't open! Using his other hand, he tried to peel them away from the bolt. But his fingers only curled more tightly around it. Had the force of the electricity within it melded it to his skin? No, he didn't feel burned or anything.

Pzzzt! The jagged bolt suddenly glowed more brightly and crackled with electric sparks.

"Get off me!" Zeus shrieked in alarm. He shook his hand hard. No luck. This bolt was stuck to him like stink on a Harpy.

Hearing a hissing sound behind him, he jumped around. Abruptly a long crack split the polished marble floor just a few feet away from him. A great puff of golden, glittery steam escaped the crack. It formed a dazzling misty cloud as it rose into the air.

A woman's voice spoke from within the mist. "Are you the one?"

Zeus squinted into the big steam cloud. It popped and winked and fizzed. Was this what magic looked like? "Who's there? Are you talking to me?" he asked.

A woman stepped out of the mist cloud. Zeus couldn't help staring at her. Her shiny

hair was black as midnight. Snowy white robes covered her from head to toe. All he could see was her face.

He couldn't see her eyes, though. Because the eyeglasses she wore were completely fogged from the glittery mist around her.

The woman's arm lifted slowly. She pointed a long finger at the thunderbolt. "Did you pull that from the stone?"

"Oh, sorry. Was it yours?" Zeus asked hopefully. "Because you can have it back. Here, take it." He held it out to her, disappointed when she didn't accept his offer.

She circled him. The cloud of mist followed her. "You are young, as in the prophecy," she said, studying him from all angles. "Yes, yes, I see," she said after a few moments. "It all makes sense now."

What made sense? Zeus wondered. And

how could she see anything at all through those foggy eyeglasses?

She put her fingertips to her forehead as if she were concentrating hard. He didn't have time for this, he thought impatiently. He had to escape those Cronies!

After setting the thunderbolt on the ground again, he stood on it this time. Then he yanked on his arm. *Rats.* He still couldn't get the bolt off.

"Your name!" the lady demanded, lowering her hands. "Is it Goose?"

"Goose? No! It's Zeus," he mumbled, embarrassed. He'd always thought his name was a little odd. Most kids in Crete were named Alexander or Nicholas or something equally cool and strong-sounding. But even the name Zeus was better than Goose!

"Ah, you must forgive me," the woman said.

As he straightened, she gave him a small bow. "I am Pythia, the oracle here at the Delphi temple. I can see the future, but sometimes my vision is blurred. Due to the mist, you understand?"

There was a loud hissing, and another cloud of steam shot up from the ground. The mist grew thicker around her.

Excitement rose in Zeus at her words. "If you can see the future, tell me this: How will I get this thunderbolt off me?"

She shook her head, her robe swaying back and forth. "That, I cannot see. For what is revealed is not mine to choose."

Zeus's stomach sank. What kind of crummy power was that?

As if she'd read his thoughts, or at least sensed his disappointment, Pythia added, "But one thing I do know: Your thunderbolt has amazing magic."

"Magic? Really?" Zeus stared at the bolt. It glowed, looking extra sparky, as if it were excited to have his attention. Interesting. He'd heard of magical things before, but he'd never seen one in action. He'd certainly never expected to *have* one. Had he been too quick to try to get rid of it?

"Only the trueborn king of the Olympians could have removed that bolt from the conestone," Pythia informed him.

King of the Olympians? Him? *This lady doesn't know what she's talking about,* thought Zeus.

He shook his head slowly. "No way," he told her. "I'm no king. I'm just a mortal kid. Maybe you should keep looking for that Goose guy. He's probably the one you want."

Although he couldn't see her eyes through those foggy specs, Zeus sensed her keen interest in him. A small silence passed, and then she said, "I have been too hasty. You are not yet ready to know all that has been prophesied. So for now let us simply call you a . . . a hero in training."

"A hero?" said Zeus. His face lit up. "Epic!" This was more like it, he thought. Heroes had cool adventures. They went on quests and did other manly stuff. "What is my quest? What important thing will you have me do?"

"Go where the cone-stone leads you," she answered.

What does that mean? Zeus wondered. Then he had a thought. Maybe this cone-stone would lead him to his parents!

But before he could ask about that, Pythia stepped backward into the mist again. "Never fear," her disembodied voice called out. "We will speak again . . . and soon."

"Wait!" Zeus leaped forward, dragging the thunderbolt after him. "I have more questions. Don't go yet!"

CHAPTER SEVEN

Mysterious Symbols

Zeus ran into the mist, searching for the oracle. But she was gone.

"What am I going to do now?" he wailed, staring at the thunderbolt. It was still dangling from his hand. "I can't walk around with this thing stuck to me for the rest of my life."

Go where the cone-stone leads you, Pythia had said. If the stone could *lead* him, it must be magic too. Like the thunderbolt. Could the magic stone help free him of this zappy, clingy bolt as well as find his parents? he wondered.

Going over to the table, Zeus walked all the way around it. He examined the cone-shaped stone atop it from all sides. There were strange black symbols on it that he hadn't noticed earlier. But he couldn't read them.

He *was* able to read the words that someone had scratched in the blank spaces between the symbols, though. He read them aloud: "Help us! We are in Cronus."

As the last word left his lips, there was a scraping sound. Then . . . *pop!* A chip of rock cracked away from the main cone-stone and fell to the ground.

It bounced across the temple floor toward the urns near the wall. Zeus went looking for the chip, dragging the bolt along with him. He was just about to give up on finding it when he heard a muffled squeak under his sandal heel. It sounded like a tiny voice!

He lifted his foot and saw the cone-stone chip lying there on the temple floor. It was oval-shaped. Zeus picked it up and studied it. It was gray and smooth, like the main stone. But it was only the size of his fist, with a small, round hole through one end. It also had some of those weird black symbols on it.

"Did you say something?" he asked it. A little embarrassed, he looked around, hoping no one had seen him talking to a rock. Luckily, he was alone inside the temple now. But he could still hear the half-giants hanging around outside on the steps, waiting for him.

When he looked back at the chip, his blue eyes widened. The symbols on it had moved around! Now they formed two words: *Find Poseidon.*

As the letters faded back into symbols again, goose bumps prickled Zeus's arms. He wasn't sure if Poseidon was a person, place, or thing, but he was excited all the same. Because he was pretty sure this cone-stone chip was sending him on a quest. Wow! Maybe he really was a hero in training!

"What and where is Poseidon?" he asked the chip. Maybe it was the name of the place where his parents were. Or maybe Poseidon was his father's name!

But no new words appeared on the chip's surface. It didn't speak, either. He asked it again. And again. But the chip wouldn't reply.

Annoyed, Zeus tossed it over his shoulder. It was just an ordinary piece of rock after all, he decided. Not magical.

"Ow-yip!" a tiny voice cried as the rock hit the floor.

Zeus rushed over to the rock and snatched it up again. "So you *did* speak."

"Uh-dip." It was almost like the chip of stone was rolling its eyes at him for being dense. But stones didn't have eyes. It was speaking some kind of foreign language he couldn't understand.

Pzzzt!

"Ow!" said Zeus. The jagged thunderbolt had shot sparks into his palm. They stung like tiny insect bites, but the pain swiftly faded.

Hmm, he thought. The chip of stone had said "ow-yip" a minute ago when he'd dropped it. Had it been saying "ow" too?

As if the bolt's sparks had sparked an idea, a light went on in his brain. He lifted the small gray rock closer. "Are you speaking Chip Latin?"

The rock stayed silent.

Maybe it hadn't understood him, thought Zeus. "Like Pig Latin," he explained. "Where you move the first letter of a word to the end of it and then add an 'ay' sound." He paused. "Only you're moving the first letter of a word to the end and adding an 'ip' sound instead. As in 'chip.' Right?"

"Ight-rip," said the chip.

Which must mean "right," Zeus decided.

Stomp! Stomp! Stomp! His eyes whipped toward the temple door. Someone was coming up the temple's front steps. Someone with big feet. Still clutching the chip, he dove under the table the cone-stone sat upon.

Luckily, the table turned out to be just tall enough for him to huddle under. He looked at the bolt. It was too big, poking out from under the tablecloth. Whoever was coming would surely see it and figure out his hiding place.

"Oh! Why can't you be *small*?" he moaned softly.

Suddenly the bolt made a crunching sound, like ice cracking on a winter pond. In an instant it shrank until it was no longer than a dagger!

The stomping crossed the temple floor toward him. The new arrivals surrounded the cone-stone. They stood so close that the toes of their sandals stuck under the tablecloth on all sides of Zeus. There were six feet in all, which meant three soldiers.

Zeus tucked himself tighter, scarcely daring to breathe. Clutching the bolt in one hand and the chip of stone in the other, he waited, trembling. Right now he didn't feel at all like a hero. Not even a hero in training!

CHAPTER EIGHT

The Big Bad Bully King

S o it's true. The magic thunderbolt is gone," Zeus heard a deep voice boom. It sounded familiar.

"Do you think that Snackboy really could have pulled it out like everyone's saying?"

Under the table, Zeus's eyes went wide. That sounded like Double Chin! And the first voice had been Lion Tattoo's. That storm must have blown their ship here extra, extra fast!

"Well, he's not here to ask. And we don't dare go back to King Cronus empty-handed," added a third voice. It was Blackbeard's.

Zeus felt the chip twitch in his palm. He looked down at it. The black symbols on it had rearranged themselves again. Now they spelled: *Danger.*

Well, that was helpful. Not! The chip hadn't told him anything he didn't *already* know. There was nowhere to run. He was surrounded.

"If there's magic in the thunderbolt, there may be magic in the cone-stone, too," Lion Tattoo mused. "King Cronus likes magic. Might toss us a coin or two for it. Let's take the stone to him."

Zeus heard a scraping noise overhead. And soon heavy footsteps thumped across the floor and left the temple.

"Young Zeus has escaped!" he heard Lion

Tattoo call to the crowd of half-giants outside. "Spread out and find him. A handsome reward will be given to he who delivers the boy to the king!"

A roar went up from the soldiers. There were more stomping sounds as they all began to leave.

Once it was quiet, Zeus crawled out from under the table. He wasn't surprised to see that the big cone-stone was gone.

He tiptoed across the temple floor. In the distance he could see Lion Tattoo and his two companions moving through the forest. They were knocking down olive trees and crushing grapevines along the way. All the other half-giants were gone too. They were searching for him when he was right here under their big noses. Ha!

Hmm. Lion Tattoo was carrying the cone-stone under one arm. Oracle Pythia had

instructed him to go where the stone led. Well then, he supposed he'd better follow!

Zeus had only taken a single step toward the door when suddenly Lion Tattoo turned and looked back toward the temple. Zeus dove behind a column, his heart hammering in his chest. Had he been seen? But when he dared to check again, none of his enemies were looking his way.

He needed to get going, before the trio of half-giants got too far ahead of him. But what if he got caught following them and was taken before the king?

Zeus hesitated, still safe behind the column. King Cronus was not a nice guy. First of all, he was a Titan. Rumor had it that Titan giants were *twice* as mean as half-giants. And Cronus was the biggest, baddest Titan of them all!

And Poseidon might actually have nothing

whatsoever to do with his parents. If so, why should he rescue this Poseidon—whoever or whatever he was? "For all I know, Poseidon could be the name of another dumb thunder-bolt," he grumbled.

"Ow!" he yelled as the bolt zapped him again. "Stop that!" This annoying thunderbolt was the cause of all his problems. It had doomed him to accept responsibilities he'd neither wanted nor asked for. Now the stone chip twitched in his palm again. It was like the chip and the bolt were both ganging up on him! He glanced down at the chip. The symbols on it had reshaped to form a new word: *Follow.*

Still Zeus hesitated. Maybe it would be smarter to hightail it back to Crete. There he could be safe and cozy again in his cave. But was that really what he wanted?

His feet began to move. Almost like they had

decided to obey the bolt and the chip on their own. Before he knew it, he was dashing down the steps. He paused at the bottom.

"Okay, feet. You win." Pulling the leather string tie from the neck of his tunic, he threaded it through the hole in the pesky chip. Then he tied the two ends of the string together so it formed a loop.

He slipped it over his head so the chip hung around his neck like an amulet. Which wasn't exactly easy to do with a thunderbolt stuck to his hand!

Immediately the chip amulet began to twitch against his chest. "Something on your mind, Chip?" Zeus asked it.

"Ing-kip an-cip ree-fip olt-bip," the stone chip informed him.

"King can free bolt," Zeus translated. Excitement filled him as he realized what that must mean. That the king knew how to make the bolt let go of him.

On the one hand, Cronus was a terrible bully. There was no telling what the king might do to him. But on the other hand, he didn't have much choice about what to do now. Because on his other hand there was a thunderbolt!

Zeus couldn't imagine going through the rest of his life—however long that might be—with a thunderbolt stuck to him. He wanted it gone!

"Well, that settles it, then." Picking up his pace, Zeus was soon hot on the trail of Lion Tattoo and his two half-giant pals.

CHAPTER NINE

Gulp!

It was almost nightfall by the time Zeus reached the king's camp. Staying hidden behind a tree, he counted six Titan giants seated around a blazing fire. They were gobbling dinner and making plans. War plans, from the sound of it.

"Under my iron fist, Earth is now right where I want it. In terrible turmoil," one of them was saying. He wore a golden crown and had an evil gleam in his eye. This had to be King Cronus himself! Especially since the cone-stone sat right beside him on the ground.

It was hard to hear the giants over the sound of their munching, slurping, and crunching. Zeus sneaked closer. As he watched, the king pulled something from his mouth. Then he tossed whatever it was onto a huge pile behind him. A pile of mortal bones!

The king rubbed his hands together in glee. "Soon we will unleash the Creatures of Chaos in each of our realms. Mortals will be quaking in their sandals like never before! Heh-heh-heh!"

No kidding, thought Zeus. In fact, his knees were already knocking, just hearing about the creatures. Weren't any of the other Titans going to stop this rotten king from putting his dastardly plans into action?

"What about the Olympians?" one of them dared to ask. His entire head glowed sort of like a pale sun. "You've failed to capture them all." The others nodded, grumbling.

King Cronus slammed a meaty fist on his knee, looking fierce. "I've captured five." For some reason, he rubbed his belly as he said this. He had the most enormous belly Zeus had ever seen. It stuck out so far over his belt that it almost covered his thighs.

"But more are still on the loose—a threat to us," another Titan argued. This one had a large pair of wings sticking out behind him. "We've heard rumors there could be as many as a dozen all together."

"If there are more, I will find them all and jail them," Cronus began.

"In your belly? No, I think it would be safer to jail them separately," the Sunhead Titan insisted. "At the far corners of the Earth. And under guard!"

Zeus gasped. So that's why Cronus's belly was so big! It was full of Olympians, whoever they were. *Yuck!*

Wait a minute! The message scratched on the cone-stone had said: *We are in Cronus!* The Olympians must've written it somehow. And Pythia had said that the king of the Olympians was supposed to pull the thunderbolt from the cone-stone. Only *Zeus* had done it instead.

What if Poseidon was the true Olympian king instead of that Goose guy? That made sense, didn't it? Why else would Chip be so anxious for Zeus to find him? Hey! If Poseidon was inside Cronus and Zeus got him out, maybe Poseidon would take this thunderbolt off his hands—um, hand.

As if it could read his mind, the thunderbolt

gave a hard jolt. Zeus heard that ice-crunching sound again. "No! Not now, Bolt!" he hissed.

But in an instant the bolt flashed to its full length. It sparked and sizzled with electricity. Unfortunately, as it expanded, it accidentally sliced through the trunk of the tree Zeus was hiding behind. It crashed to the ground, barely missing him.

The twelve giants' heads whipped around to stare in his direction.

"Who's there?" demanded Cronus, leaping to his feet. Standing tall, he looked even more terrifying than he had while seated.

"Small! Small!" Zeus hissed urgently. At his command the bolt shrank again. He wasn't quite ready to meet the king after all, he decided. He whirled around to run.

But before he could take a step, something poked through the back of his tunic. "Gotcha,

Snackboy!" He was yanked upward on the tip of a spear. Lion Tattoo's spear. Double Chin and Blackbeard stood beside him, grinning.

Zeus had been so busy spying, he hadn't noticed the half-giants sneaking up on him. As he dangled in midair, the half-giants carried him over to the Titans sitting around the fire.

He felt the chip amulet shudder against his chest. Quickly he tucked it inside the neck of his tunic, where it couldn't be seen.

"We have found Zeus, Your Majesty!" Lion Tattoo announced, bowing on one knee. Lowering the angle of the spear, he dropped Zeus before the king. The half-giants looked at the king expectantly, obviously hoping for a reward. They frowned mightily when Cronus merely waved them away.

Meanwhile, Zeus had landed on all fours at Cronus's feet. The Titans closed in around him.

Suddenly it began to snow. *Huh? It's not winter,* thought Zeus. And why was it snowing around him but nowhere else?

He tasted one of the snowflakes. Salt! Looking up, he saw the king's giant hand hovering above him. He was pouring salt out of a glass shaker. Onto *him.*

As far as Zeus knew, the only things that got salted were slugs and dinner. He wasn't a slug. Which meant Cronus must be planning to make him—*Yikes!*

"Why does everyone want to eat me today?" Zeus complained.

Peering down at him over his great big belly, Cronus laughed. "Heh-heh-heh! This one's funny."

Zeus leaped to his feet, brushing salt from his hair. "Release Poseidon!" he demanded.

The king laughed even harder, slapping his knee. "Yeah, right! You are one hilarious kid.

It's gonna be fun having you around for an eternity." Plucking Zeus up by the back of his tunic, he lifted him high overhead.

Cronus tilted his head back. "Over the teeth and past the gums, look out, belly, here Zeus comes!" His giant mouth opened wide.

From somewhere down below, Zeus heard voices. They sounded like they were coming from deep in a cave. Or from inside Cronus's belly!

"Let us out! Help! Can you hear us?"

The Olympians! Was Poseidon among them? If he could somehow make the bolt let go, and if he could somehow trick Cronus into swallowing it, maybe Poseidon would catch it and fight his way out. Then the thunderbolt could be *his* problem instead of Zeus's.

Without warning, Cronus's fingers released him. Zeus fell feetfirst straight toward a gaping black pit full of teeth. *Nooo!* He wanted Cronus to swallow the bolt, not swallow him!

In the nick of time Zeus spread his legs. He landed with his feet braced on either side of Cronus's nose. A big tongue swiped around, reaching for him. *It's now or never,* he thought desperately.

Drawing back one arm, Zeus yelled, "Fly!" He hurled the bolt down the Titan giant's throat. Then he looked down at his hand, hardly able to believe it. The thunderbolt had obeyed him. It was gone!

The giant's eyes widened. His mouth snapped shut as if he'd accidentally swallowed a bug. A *lightning* bug! His face turned red, and he wrapped his hands around his own throat. He swayed, like a giant oak tree in a storm.

Zeus lost his footing and tumbled backward. He began to fall. Catching a button on the front of Cronus's tunic, he hung on for dear life.

"Wait! I know what to do!" Sunhead ran to

stand behind Cronus. He wrapped his beefy arms around his chest, just above the spot where Zeus was hanging. Sunhead linked his fists over the king's solar plexus. Then he pulled, hard.

King Cronus turned a sickly green. And then suddenly . . . *BLEAEAH!* He barfed! Big time.

A huge stream of ookiness blasted out of his mouth like water from a fountain. Only it wasn't water. It was gross stuff. The force of it slammed into Zeus, knocking him toward the ground. He slid down Cronus's belly like it was a vomit slide.

Sploosh! Zeus fell into the big barf swamp that was forming at the king's feet. It was a swirling mess of epic proportions. There were beast bones, unidentifiable gloppy goo, and five lumps. The lumps were each about the same size as Zeus. And they were moving!

Zeus stood up. Or tried to. He kept sliding and landing on his butt again.

"Eew!" a voice shrieked. "This is disgusting!" It was a girl. She was slipping and sliding too. Despite the goo that covered her, Zeus could see that her long hair was golden. And her eyes were as blue as his own.

Meanwhile, Cronus was moaning and holding his stomach. Seeming to all of a sudden figure out what had happened, he managed to yell, "Get them!"

Then things happened fast. The Titan giants began grabbing up the lumps. One giant snatched up the cone-stone, too.

Zeus tried to get to his feet. He had to fight the giants off! But just as one of them reached for him, Zeus was swept downhill. Carried off on a whooshing river of yuck. At the bottom of the hill he slammed into a rock.

Instantly everything went dark, and he knew no more.

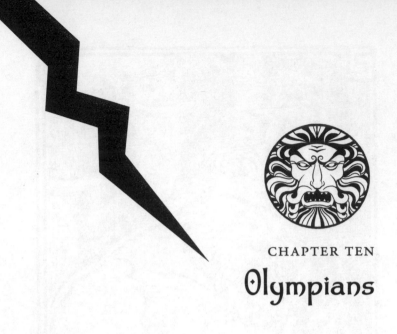

CHAPTER TEN

Olympians

P.u. Something stinks!" Zeus said woozily.

"It's you," said a girl's voice. "I've already bathed in the waterfall."

Zeus remembered that voice. The girl with the long golden hair!

Suddenly everything came back to him. He leaped to his feet, looking around for the Titans. It was morning. He was at the bottom of a hill, surrounded by enormous boulders and trees. He'd slid a long way from where the Titans had built their fire. King Cronus and the others were nowhere in sight.

He sniffed himself. The stink was definitely him. *Ugh.* At least he was finally free of the thunderbolt. He looked around again, making sure it wasn't sneaking up on him or anything. Was it still in Cronus's belly, or—

"So he's finally awake?" asked a boy's voice.

Zeus turned his head to see a boy with turquoise eyes coming toward them. The girl and the boy were both about his age, as far as he could tell. "You wouldn't be Poseidon by any chance?" Zeus asked the boy.

"Who wants to know?" asked the girl.

But the boy nodded at the same time. "Yeah, I am. And she's Hera."

"Yes!" said Zeus, pumping a fist. Despite all

that had gone wrong, he'd managed to succeed in his first quest. He'd followed the cone-stone and found Poseidon. Turned out Poseidon was a kid, not his dad. It was disappointing, but finding his parents would just have to wait.

"What's your name?" Hera demanded.

"Zeus."

Hera and Poseidon gave each other a startled look. "Isn't that the name Cronus called out before he swallowed the cone-st—" Poseidon started to say. Hera elbowed him before he could finish.

"Swallowed what?" Zeus asked.

Hera put on a fake kind of smile. "Oh, nothing. How did you find us, anyway?"

"I was sent here to rescue you. By an oracle. And by *this*." Zeus lifted the chip amulet that hung around his neck.

Poseidon stepped closer to examine it, then fanned his face. "Maybe you should take a shower before we talk." He pointed toward the waterfall beyond some trees nearby.

Quickly Zeus went to bathe in the waterfall and wash his tunic. Afterward he put his wet tunic and sandals back on.

When he returned to his companions, he explained everything. He told them all that had happened to him since leaving Crete. Including how Pythia had called him a hero in training.

"Well, she sure got that wrong," Hera scoffed.

"Gosh, don't try to spare my feelings or anything," said Zeus.

"No, I just meant—" She glanced at Poseidon. "Think we can trust him?"

Poseidon shrugged. "Your call."

Hera studied Zeus intently, then shook her head. "No, I don't think we'll trust you quite yet. You could be one of Cronus's spies."

"I'm not!" Zeus insisted.

"You can prove it to us, then," she said.

"How?"

"There were three more of us imprisoned in Cronus's belly," Hera told him. "Hestia, Demeter, and Hades. We escaped, but the Titan giants made off with the others. If you help us rescue them, we'll tell you a secret. A big one."

They'd been captive in a belly for ten years. What kind of secrets could they know? wondered Zeus. "King Cronus said you're Olympians. What's that?" he asked.

"We don't actually know," Poseidon replied.

"But it's something the king is afraid of," added Hera. "So that must mean we have some kind of magic powers."

"If only we knew how to use them!" said Poseidon.

With a loud rumble, the ground next to them

suddenly split open. Zeus, Hera, and Poseidon jumped back. A cloud of glittery mist appeared. Pythia's face glowed within it.

"It's her! It's the oracle I told you about!" Zeus exclaimed.

"Trouble, trouble, boil, and bubble!" the oracle murmured. "You must find the trident. One that will point the way to those you seek. One that—in the right hands—has the power to defeat the first of the king's Creatures of Chaos."

As quickly as the mist appeared, it disappeared again.

"Huh? Which hands are the right hands?" asked Poseidon.

"Probably mine," Zeus and Hera said at the same time.

Zeus rolled his eyes. He'd grown up around girls. But the nymph, the bee, and the goat who'd raised him had always let him have his way. He had a feeling this girl was going to be different.

"Come on, let's get going," Poseidon said. "See that hill over there? Maybe if we climb to the top, we can figure out which way to go."

"So we're supposed to find a trident," said Zeus as they started to walk. "Shouldn't be too hard."

Hera and Poseidon nodded. The three continued on for a bit without saying anything more. Finally Zeus said, "One question. What's a trident?"

Hera and Poseidon both shrugged. "No idea," they admitted at the same time.

"Well, I do know that 'tri' means 'three,'" said Hera.

"Like us?" said Poseidon. "There are three of us."

It wasn't much of a clue. Zeus frowned. How

were they going to find the trident when they didn't even know what it was? An hour later they reached the top of the hill.

Hera gasped. "Look!" On the distant horizon they saw land's end. Beyond it the entire sea was boiling.

Zeus felt his skin prickle. He repeated the oracle's words. "Trouble, trouble, boil, and bubble." Then he added, "I have a feeling that's where we'll find the trident. Our journey could be dangerous, though. Are we up for this?"

Hera lifted her chin. "Of course."

Poseidon nodded, but he looked a little nervous. "I hope the trident's not in that sea. I don't know how to swim."

Overhead the clouds darkened suddenly. The air crackled. *Uh-oh!* Zeus knew what that meant. But before he could warn his new friends—

Ka-pow!

The thunderbolt was back! It stood before him, crackling and sparking. He started to run downhill trying to get away from it. The bolt chased him.

"Small!" Zeus commanded, breathlessly coming to a stop at the bottom of the hill. In a flash the thunderbolt shrank to the size of a dagger. It hovered in the air before him, darting around as if wanting to be held. Zeus thrust his hands under his armpits so that the bolt couldn't get to them.

It buzzed around him, looking for a way in. Finally seeming to give up, it slid under the belt at the waist of his tunic. At least it hadn't managed to get stuck to his hand again.

"Good Bolt," said Zeus as Hera and Poseidon caught up to him. "Stay."

Poseidon's eyebrows went up in awe. "You have a thunderbolt for a pet?"

"Seems like it," said Zeus. "C'mon. Let's get going."

Hera rolled her eyes. "Who made you boss, Thunderboy?"

"Thunderboy?" Zeus echoed. He liked the sound of that.

Beyond the hill, he could feel the sea calling to him. Could feel his destiny beckon.

"Follow me," he said more firmly. And to his surprise, they did. With long, confident strides, he led the others toward the boiling sea.

Poseidon and the Sea of Fury

For our heroic husbands:

Mark Williams
—S. W.

George Hallowell
—J. H.

Greetings,
Mortal Readers,

I am Pythia, the Oracle of Delphi, in Greece. I have the power to see the future. Hear my prophecy:

Ahead, I see dancers lurking. Wait—make that *danger* lurking. (The future can be blurry, especially when my eyeglasses are foggy.)

Anyhoo, beware! Titan giants now rule all of Earth's domains—oceans, mountains, forests, and the depths of the Underwear. Oops—make that *Underworld*. Led by King Cronus, they are out to destroy us all!

Yet I foresee hope. A band of rightful rulers called Olympians will arise. Though their size and youth are no match for the Titans, they will be giant in heart, mind, and spirit. They await their leader—a very special, yet clueless godboy. One who is destined to become king of the gods and ruler of the heavens.

If he is brave enough.

And if he accepts that sometimes he must share the cage—um—*stage* with fiends. Oops. *Friends!*

For only by working together will these young rulers-to-be have a chance at saving the world.

CHAPTER ONE

Under Attack!

A spear whizzed by ten-year-old Zeus's ear. He ducked his head but didn't stop running. Neither did his two companions, Hera and Poseidon. They were right behind him.

"Halt in your tracks or you're dead meat, Snackboy!" a cruel voice boomed.

He'd know that voice anywhere. It was Lion Tattoo. That was what Zeus had nicknamed him, anyway. He was the leader of the three half-giants who were after Zeus. They were soldiers in King Cronus's army and stood as tall as trees.

Just three days before, they'd snatched Zeus from his cave in Crete and brought him here to Greece. He'd already escaped them—twice. But he might not be so lucky a third time.

"When we catch you, we *will* eat you!" hollered a second voice. Blackbeard's. Another of the half-giants.

Then the third one—Zeus had dubbed him Double Chin—added his two cents. "Yeah! And we'll chomp your friends for dessert! Ha-ha-ha!" He followed this up with a loud burp.

A shiver ran down Zeus's spine. They were probably bluffing, though. Their orders were more likely to take him, Hera, and Poseidon back to King Cronus. So that the *king* could swallow them whole!

They approached a ditch. Zeus jumped in and hunkered down, waiting for Hera and Poseidon to catch up. Within seconds Hera dropped in to crouch beside him.

"We'll never reach the sea at this rate. Somebody else is going to find that trident thingie before we do. Do something, Thunderboy!" she hissed.

Zeus liked the nickname she'd given him. But she sure did know how to make it sound like an insult sometimes.

"Don't be so impatient. We'll get there," he told her. "We're on a quest, remember? You can't expect it to be fast or easy."

An oracle named Pythia had sent them on this quest to search for a magical trident. Which was going to be a challenge, since none of them knew what a trident was. But they did know their destination—the sea.

Just then Poseidon dove between them, thumping their shoulders as he fell.

"Ow!" Zeus and Hera complained at the same time.

"Half-giant soldiers? This is all we need," Poseidon complained back. "My feet are killing me."

Zeus's were too. No wonder. In the past two days they'd journeyed over hills, across valleys, and through forests.

Hera rolled her eyes at Poseidon. "Wuss."

"I am *not* a wuss!" he objected. "I'm an Olympian."

"Well, then act like one," Hera snapped.

"What makes you the boss of how Olympians act?" Poseidon snapped back.

"I'm an Olympian too, remember?" said Hera. "You don't hear *me* whining."

"Would you two stop arguing for half a second?" Zeus pleaded. "Those soldiers are going to hear you." Hera and Poseidon had been fighting almost the entire trip!

"I don't hear anything," Poseidon whispered a few minutes later. "Think we lost them?"

Hera peeked out of the ditch. "The coast looks clear. So what now?" They both looked at Zeus.

Zeus lifted the amulet that was strung on a leather cord around his neck. He'd found it at the temple in Delphi. He studied the amulet, a chip of rock about the size of his fist.

"Which way?" he asked it.

The strange black symbols on the chip's smooth, gray surface began to move around. Acting like a compass, they formed an arrow pointing east.

"That way," Zeus told the others. Hopping out of the ditch, he was off again. Hera and Poseidon followed.

But no sooner had all three left their hidey-hole than another spear whizzed over their heads. *"Yeeoch!"* It came so close it nearly parted Zeus's dark hair.

"Fee, fi, fo, fum. Look out, Snacklets. Here we come!" *Stomp, stomp, stomp.* It was the unmistakable sound of half-giant sandals pounding toward them.

"They're baaack!" shouted Zeus. He and Hera took off, running neck and neck.

Poseidon surged past them. His turquoise eyes were round with fear. And he seemed to have forgotten all about his feet hurting.

Hearing a *caw* overhead, Zeus glanced up. A seagull circled above them. He pointed at it. "We must," he said, panting, "be getting close to the sea."

He was right. Around the next bend in the road, they spotted the Aegean Sea off to their left. It was bright blue and dotted with little islands. Weird, wispy steam rose from its surface. Its waters churned and bubbled.

Zeus recalled the oracle's words—words that had prompted their quest and led them to this sea: *Trouble, trouble, boil, and bubble! You must find the trident. One that will point the way to those you seek. One that—in the right hands—has the power to defeat the first of the king's Creatures of Chaos.*

Hera glanced down at the sea as she ran. "I hope we make it that far," she said breathlessly.

Just then a sharp electric jolt zapped Zeus in the ribs. "Ow!" he yelled. But the jolt reminded him that he *did* have a weapon to use against the soldiers.

"You guys keep going!" he called to Hera. "I'll catch up later!"

"Okay!" Hera's long, golden hair whipped in the wind as she kept running.

Zeus slowed, reaching for his zigzag dagger. It was tucked under the belt at his waist. He freed it, then spoke a command. "Large!"

With a sound like the crunching of a glacier, the bolt expanded. In an instant it became a glowing thunderbolt as tall as Zeus. It sparked and sizzled with electric energy.

Grasping it tightly, Zeus drew it back. Then he sent it soaring. "Zap them, Bolt!" Immediately the thunderbolt took off after Hera and Poseidon.

"No! Not *them*," Zeus called in the nick of time. "The Cronies!" That was what everyone called King Cronus's soldiers. Not to their faces, though, because they didn't like it one bit.

The bolt screeched to a halt in midair. Then it switched directions and buzzed off toward the soldiers. Zeus ran the other way to catch up with Hera and Poseidon. He would have to be

more exact in his commands from now on. He'd nearly fried his friends!

Zzzpt! "Ow!" *Zzzpt!* "Ow!" The air behind him was soon filled with yelps and curses. Bolt was zapping one soldier after another.

Then Lion Tattoo's voice rang out, "Retreat!"

CHAPTER TWO

Sea Journey

Zeus laughed as the sound of the half-giants' stomping sandals grew distant. "Ha! Take that!" he yelled. Lion Tattoo pretended to be fierce, but he'd been afraid of a little bee back at Zeus's cave on Crete. A thunderbolt must seem a hundred times more terrifying to him.

Zeus jogged down the steep, rocky hillside. Below him fishermen were mending nets on the shore. Hera and Poseidon were there too, waiting on a dock overlooking the sea.

Zeus could hear the roar and crash of waves as he moved lower. This was one angry sea!

Just as he reached the beach, his thunderbolt zoomed back. Shrinking to dagger size, it slid into place beneath his belt.

"Good boy, Bolt," Zeus told it. Happy little sparks sizzled from between his fingers as he gave it a pat. The thunderbolt glowed with pride.

To think that he'd once been desperate to get rid of it! He'd found it stuck in a huge cone-shaped stone on display at the temple in Delphi. It was the same temple where he'd first met Pythia, the oracle.

After he'd pulled the thunderbolt out, it had stuck to his hand like glue. He had tried everything to get rid of it. Nothing had worked.

He'd had a good reason for not wanting to

keep it. It *scared* him. He'd been struck by lightning dozens of times back on Crete, and it wasn't fun. But now that he'd realized Bolt wasn't out to zap him, they were getting to be, well, friends. It was a little worrisome.

"Don't get too attached to me," he warned the bolt. "Because you're not really mine. Pythia said you belong to some guy named Goose. He's destined to become king of the Olympians."

After crossing the beach, Zeus stepped off the sand onto the wooden dock. Being king of the Olympians wasn't a job he'd want. This Goose guy was going to have his hands full—whenever Zeus found him. After all, Hera and Poseidon were Olympians. Ruling over them would be a pain in the butt!

"Soldiers gone?" Poseidon asked as Zeus came up to him and Hera. The three of them eyed the hillside where they'd been attacked.

"For now, anyway," Zeus replied. "But more will come."

"Then let's get out of here," Hera said impatiently. "Any idea where to start looking for this so-called trident?"

At her question the chip amulet around Zeus's neck twitched. He looked down at it. The black symbols had formed a new arrow. This one pointed straight off the end of the dock toward the sea. Zeus held the amulet up so Hera and Poseidon could see it too.

"So we're supposed to dive into the sea? And just start randomly searching?" Hera asked skeptically.

Poseidon's eyes went wide. "No," he said, backing away. "I can't swim! And if I fall into seawater, I'll—I'll melt!"

Hera frowned. "Wuss," she taunted. "It's pointing to the sea. We have to go."

Zeus held his ears. He wasn't used to so much blabbering. Until three days ago he'd lived a boring life in his quiet cave on Crete with a silent nymph, a bee, and a goat.

"Did you fight like this the whole time you were in the king's belly?" Zeus asked with a frown. But his companions were arguing too loudly to hear him. He sometimes couldn't help wondering if freeing them had been a mistake!

He could still picture how surprised King Cronus had looked when Zeus had thrown his thunderbolt down the king's throat. How the giant Titan king's face had turned red as he'd choked. And then green as he'd barfed up Poseidon, Hera, and three more Olympians— two girls and a boy.

Zeus couldn't remember the names of those three now. They had been quickly recaptured by King Cronus and his Titan buddies.

The bickering slowed, and Zeus let go of his ears. He was just in time to hear a tiny voice pipe up. "Hip-sip," it said.

Startled, Hera and Poseidon jumped. Then they stared at the amulet, since that's where the voice had come from. "Did that thing just talk?" Hera asked.

Zeus nodded. "Guess I forgot to tell you it does that."

"'Hip-sip'?" said Poseidon. "What's that mean?"

"It's Chip Latin," Zeus explained. "Like Pig Latin. Only, you move the first letter of a word to the end and add an 'ip' sound instead. As in 'chip.'"

"So 'hip-sip' means '*ship*'!" Hera exclaimed. "Where can we get one?" She looked at the amulet as if waiting for a reply. But the chip of stone was silent.

Zeus shrugged. "Guess we're supposed to figure that part out on our own."

"Oh." A look of intense concentration came over Hera's face. She squeezed her forehead with her fingertips.

"What are you doing?" Zeus asked.

"Trying to use my magic powers to get us a ship. If you can command a magic thunderbolt, it must mean Poseidon and I can do magic too. After all, we're all O— Ow!"

Poseidon had just elbowed her sharply, shaking his head.

"We're all what?" asked Zeus, looking from one to the other of them.

"Nothing," she said, looking away.

"Hera and I don't know for sure that we have magic powers," Poseidon explained. "All we know is that King Cronus fears us. And the others."

The other three Olympians who'd been in Cronus's belly, he meant. Who knew where they were now.

"He may fear you," Zeus said, "but I think he fears *me*, too. Just wish I knew why."

Hera and Poseidon traded secretive looks. Before Zeus could open his mouth to ask what *that* was all about, a fisherman came by. "Looking for transport?" he asked them.

When they nodded, he led them to a small sailing ship about ten feet long. "It washed up onshore this morning," he told them. "No one's claimed it, so you're welcome to it. But you're crazy if you go out in these rough seas. I've never seen them this angry."

"Look at the name painted on the side!" said Poseidon, pointing to the boat. "No way. I'm not getting into a boat named *Sinker*!" He backed away.

Zeus peered more closely at the painted lettering. "Wait! There's a *t* that's faded out. So it's not named *Sinker*; it's—"

"Stinker?" finished Hera doubtfully. "Oh, much better."

Zeus didn't like to rush into things, so he walked around the boat, studying it. It looked a bit leaky, but it would have to do.

They thanked the fisherman and bid him good-bye. Then they shoved the *Stinker* into the water and hopped aboard.

And they were off. Into the furious sea!

CHAPTER THREE

Fiiissshh

"A nybody know how to steer a boat?"
Zeus asked once they'd set sail.

Poseidon didn't answer. Struck dumb
with terror, he was gazing at the steaming, boiling sea around them.

"I'm sure I can figure it out," said Hera,
brimming with confidence. She stood to go
to the tiller, a lever used to turn the boat.
"Yikes!" She stumbled when a wave knocked

them unexpectedly. Then she toppled over the side!

"She'll be boiled alive!" Poseidon shrieked.

When she bobbed to the surface again, Zeus grabbed her arm. He and Poseidon reeled her back into the boat.

"Weird," Hera said once she was inside. "The water's not that hot, even though it's boiling."

"Hmm. Maybe its fury is just meant to scare people off," said Zeus. "To keep them away from the sea, so they won't come searching for the trident."

Taking the tiller, he figured out the basics of sailing after a few tries. To go in the direction the chip amulet pointed, he actually had to move the tiller the opposite direction.

Hera and Poseidon managed to angle the sail into the wind. Soon they were speeding over the choppy sea.

"I feel seasick," Poseidon complained after a while.

"Then hang your head over the side of the ship!" Hera said in alarm.

Poseidon leaned over the ship's bow and threw up. "Hey, I feel a lot better now," he said after he straightened again. "In fact, I'm hungry."

"Me too," said Zeus. His stomach was growling. Except for a few apples they'd snatched from an orchard that morning, they hadn't eaten all day.

Hera looked at Zeus. "The sea must be full of fish. Maybe you could spear one with your thunderbolt?"

Zeus put a protective hand over Bolt. He stared at Hera in horror. "Are you kidding? If this thunderbolt gets wet, it could electrocute us all!"

Hera was smart about some things. But she obviously didn't know that lightning and water don't mix.

Poseidon licked his lips. "Fiiissshh," he said dreamily. He stretched his arms out in front of him. "I wish I could catch one right now."

To everyone's astonishment, a huge silver fish suddenly leaped out of the water. *Thump!* It landed neatly in Poseidon's outstretched arms. He staggered backward under its weight.

"Whoa!" Zeus caught hold of Poseidon's tunic before he could topple overboard too.

"Fiddling fishscales! That was close," said Poseidon. He gazed at the water with renewed fear.

After Zeus broiled the fish with his thunderbolt, the three ate their fill. "Yum!" Poseidon pronounced, licking his fingers. "I could eat seafood every day of the week."

"It's good," said Hera, "but I wouldn't eat it *every* day."

"Me? I'm on a seafood diet," said Zeus. "When I see food, I eat it!"

The three of them laughed. For the first time since meeting the two Olympians, Zeus almost felt like they could become friends. But then again, maybe he only felt that way because his belly was full. And because no one was chasing them. Not at the moment, anyway.

Little did he know that this peace wouldn't last long.

Keeping an eye on the direction the amulet's arrow was pointing, Zeus adjusted the tiller. The Aegean Sea continued to boil and bubble. The wind blew steadily as they forged ahead.

And then they began to see the shipwrecks. Dozens of them. Ships, dinghies, sailboats—all dashed upon the rocky islands they passed. The sea's fury had done this!

"Tell me about the other Olympians," Zeus

suggested. He wanted to keep them all from thinking about the possibility that they might accidentally wind up wrecked too. "The ones that were with you in King Cronus's belly. What were their names again?"

"Hestia, Demeter, and Hades," said Hera. "Girl, girl, boy," she added in case the names were unfamiliar to him.

Zeus nodded. "I still don't get why Cronus swallowed all of you, though."

"Duh. To keep us imprisoned," said Poseidon.

"Because he fears your magic powers?" Zeus asked. "But why does he think they're dangerous to him? I mean, you don't even know what they are, much less how to use them."

Hera and Poseidon exchanged a guarded look.

"All right," Zeus said. "What's the big secret?" Before they'd started their journey, Hera had said she had one, but she wouldn't tell him what it was. Because she suspected he might be one of Cronus's spies!

"Look," he said. "I helped you escape. What more proof do you need that I'm on your side?"

"The trident," Hera said stubbornly.

Poseidon nodded.

Zeus opened his mouth to argue.

"Shh!" Poseidon interrupted. "Do you hear that?"

Zeus and Hera cocked their heads to listen too. The sound of harp music and beautiful singing filled the air.

"I wonder where it's coming from," Zeus said. He peered through the veil of steam.

"Over there!" Poseidon said excitedly. He pointed toward a tiny island surrounded by jagged rocks and cliffs.

Suddenly Zeus didn't care about finding the

trident anymore. He just wanted to get near the music.

"Let's go in for a closer look," Poseidon suggested.

"Great idea," said Zeus. He shifted the tiller, turning the ship toward the island. The arrow on the chip amulet was pointing in the opposite direction, but he ignored it.

The steam slowly lifted. There were three women perched on the rocks! They were dressed in flowing robes and had wings.

As the three women strummed their harps and sang, Zeus was filled with an intense longing for family. For the parents he'd never known. They'd abandoned him in the cave. Why?

Somehow he felt that these women could tell him. *We have all the answers,* their song seemed to say.

Hera pointed to Zeus's amulet. "Stop! Chip wants us to turn around."

Zeus looked down. The amulet's arrow was glowing red now. It flashed on and off pointing them *away* from the island. Still Zeus ignored it and steered directly for the rocks.

"Got to get closer," he murmured.

"Must. Listen. Forever," Poseidon added in a dreamy voice.

"What's wrong with you?" Hera asked, looking between them worriedly. She snapped her fingers in Zeus's face, but he didn't even blink. And Poseidon seemed just as far gone.

"I think those women and their rock music have put you both under a magic spell!" she said. "Only, for some reason it's not affecting me."

As if in a trance, Zeus steered the *Stinker* even closer. "Anger-dip!" shrieked the chip. Which meant "danger." But Zeus paid no attention. His head was full of music.

All at once the song changed and sounded more sinister. A huge wave swelled behind them. It began pushing the ship straight for the jagged rocks.

The song ended. The women started cackling.

"Look out!" screamed Hera. "We're going to crash!"

CHAPTER FOUR

Sea Serpents and Merpeople

Suddenly the boat gave a hard jerk. Zeus and Poseidon bumped heads. "Ow!" They exclaimed at the same time. Freed from the song's spell, Zeus shook his head dizzily. He felt like he'd just awakened from a dream. One that had turned into a nightmare!

He and Poseidon sprang into action, trying to help Hera get control of the ship. It creaked and groaned as the giant wave pushed it. The rocks loomed closer. And closer.

Just as the *Stinker* was about to be splintered into toothpicks, two sea serpents rose from the water. They were as big as half-giants and had tails twice the length of the sailboat.

One of the serpents curled its scaly blue-green tail under the ship and tossed it high. The other did an expert twist. With a flip of his tail, he batted the boat away from the rocks.

"Hold on!" yelled Zeus as the *Stinker* went whirling through the air. Seconds later it splashed down so hard that it nearly fell apart. But somehow it landed upright and intact, with the three of them still safely inside.

Hera got up from the bottom of the boat where she'd fallen. "Why did you listen to those singers?" she demanded.

"Um," Zeus said.

"Uh, well," said Poseidon.

The two sea serpents overheard and swam up to them. "Don't blame yourselves. Those were Sirens," one of them said. "Their beautiful music lures sailors to their deaths. *Boy* sailors, that is."

"So there," Poseidon said to Hera. "They put us under a magic spell."

"Yeah, we couldn't help it," said Zeus.

"Whatever." Hera's eyes flicked to the sea serpents. Before anyone could thank them for their good deed, they dipped their heads in a farewell bow. Then they turned and glided off.

"Did you see how those serpents were staring at me?" Poseidon asked. "It was like they knew me or something."

"What? You're crazy," scoffed Hera. "They were looking at all of us."

"Maybe," said Zeus. But it seemed to him that they really might've been staring extra hard at Poseidon. *Strange.*

Poseidon shivered. "Well, the sooner we find that trident thing and get out of this creepy sea, the better."

"Agreed." Zeus checked the chip's arrow, which was black again. Then he moved the tiller to take them in the right direction.

Night fell and they sailed on. Two more sunless days and starless nights passed. They took turns sleeping and manning the tiller and the sail.

When it rained, they collected fresh water in a bucket they'd found onboard. And every time they grew hungry, Poseidon had only to say, "I wish for fish." Immediately a fish would leap into his arms.

"Why don't you try wishing for something else to leap into your arms next time?" Hera suggested to him one morning. "Like a trident."

Poseidon nodded. "I already thought of that. Only it didn't work." His eyes got big as he stared at something beyond Zeus. *"Flipping fish-heads!* Who are they?"

Zeus looked in the direction Poseidon was gazing. Three heads were peeking up over the ship's stern. They giggled in what sounded like children's voices. But they weren't children. One had a beard. And they all had turquoise eyes like Poseidon's.

"So it's true," the bearded one said. He was staring at Poseidon in awe. "The sea serpents told us you would come one day. We've waited a long time. Have you come to rescue the sea?"

Poseidon blinked. "Who, me?"

"Who are you?" Hera asked them.

"Not exactly," Zeus answered. They'd all spoken at the same time.

"We're merpeople," replied one of the creatures. The three of them were now swimming gracefully around the ship.

"Well, we're here to search for a trident," Zeus told him. "Have you seen one?"

"Sure. Got one right here." The bearded merman held up a three-pronged spear. It looked sort of like a pitchfork, only cooler.

Zeus's eyes lit up. Could it be this easy? Had they already found the magic trident?

But then the other two held up tridents of their own. "Every merperson has one," said a mergirl with long pink hair.

"Is there a special one somewhere, though?" Zeus asked.

All three merpeople nodded. "Oceanus has the mightiest of them all," said the merman. "Fearsome what it can do!"

"Where can we find him?" Zeus asked quickly.

The merpeople huddled close, looking scared at the very idea. "You must not get around much. Where are you from?" the merman asked.

"Belly," Hera and Poseidon said together before Zeus could answer.

The merpeople glanced at Poseidon, appearing intrigued.

Zeus shrugged. "Cave," he said. It was hard to learn much when you were raised in places like that, but they were trying to make up for lost time.

The merman zoomed backward on his tail, then dove with a splash. When he came up again, he said, "Oceanus pretty much rules the sea. He could be anywhere in it."

"Is he a friend of King Cronus's?" asked Hera.

The merpeople looked even more fearful at the mention of the king. "Probably," the mergirl told them. "Those twelve Titans usually stick together."

"Oceanus is a Titan?" gasped Hera.

"Twelve!" Zeus echoed. He'd only seen *six* Titans that night he'd met Cronus.

It seemed pretty clear to him that Oceanus's

trident must be the one they sought. But just how they were going to get it from a Titan, he had no idea. If they told him Pythia wanted them to have it, would he just hand it over? Not likely!

"Where can we find him?" Zeus asked again.

"*You* don't find *him*," the merman said. "*He* finds *you*. If you're very unlucky, that is."

The younger green-haired mergirl nodded. "Instead of looking for him, you should turn around and sail as far south as possible."

"Because that's where he lives?" asked Poseidon.

The merpeople sent him another strange look. Then they giggled again.

"No," said the merman. "Because it's the best way to avoid being buried at sea."

Hera glared at Poseidon. "I think they mean we go north to find him, Doofus-eidon."

CHAPTER FIVE

Trident Trouble

How do we know for sure it's Oceanus's trident we're after?" Hera argued as Zeus steered their boat north.

He tacked left and their boat sped over the waves. "You heard what the merman said. It's fearsome and mighty. It *must* be magic."

If he didn't know any better, he'd think Hera was scared to meet Oceanus. But then, why wouldn't she be? Titans were bad news. Still, getting the trident was the whole point of their quest!

Hera frowned. "Pythia didn't actually *say* that the trident is magical. She just said it will *point the way to those we seek*. 'To the lost Olympians' is what she meant."

Or to my parents, Zeus thought. Finding them was his constant hope, even though he had no idea who or where his parents were.

"Maybe one trident is as good as another," Hera went on. "I think we should go back and find those merpeople again. They seemed friendly. I bet one of them would let us borrow a trident."

Poseidon grinned at Hera. "Cluck, cluck," he said, flapping his arms like wings. "I think someone's chickening out."

"Am not!" Hera protested hotly. Balling her

hands into fists, she stomped toward Poseidon, rocking the ship.

"Stop! I told you I'll melt if I fall into the water!" he squealed.

"Promise?" Hera countered with a too-sweet smile. But she left him alone and sat down.

"Let's think this out," Zeus said, hoping to stop their fighting. "Pythia said the trident has the power to defeat the first of the king's Creatures of Chaos. Don't you think a trident powerful enough to do that would have to be magical?"

"I'd think so," Poseidon said smugly.

"Maybe," said Hera. "But she said the trident only has power if it's *in the right hands*. What if my hands are the right ones? Maybe *I* can use one of the merpeople's tridents to defeat these so-called Creatures of Chaos—whatever they are."

"So go back," suggested Poseidon. He grinned at Zeus. "We won't stop her, will we?"

"It's Oceanus's trident we want," Zeus said. "I'm almost sure of it."

Hera crossed her arms. "Look, Mr. Bossy Thunderpants. I demand that you turn this boat around and go find those merpeople."

Zeus couldn't believe her nerve. And she thought *he* was bossy! "We'll lose time if we backtrack now," he told her. The wind was blowing steadily, and they'd already left the merpeople far behind. "I say we go on."

Hera glared at him. "And I say—"

"Look! Dolphins!" interrupted Poseidon, pointing off to the right. A pod of them were leaping in the waves. Their slick silver sides flashed as they dove and then resurfaced.

He sent Hera a mischievous look. "I think you should catch a ride back with one of them.

Then Zeus and I could have some peace." No sooner had the words left his mouth, than one of the dolphins headed toward them.

Zeus, Hera, and Poseidon watched in amazement as it drew up alongside the ship. Fixing an eye on Hera, it chattered at her as if inviting her onto its back.

"See?" said Hera. "This proves I'm right to go back. Even that dolphin knows it!"

The dolphin kept on chattering, but now it was eyeing Poseidon. "Don't look at me," he said, sitting down. "I'm staying put."

But Hera climbed over the side of the boat and straddled the dolphin's back. "As soon as I have the trident, I'll come find you," she told the boys. "If Oceanus doesn't find you first. I mean, you might be hard to locate if you're fish food at the bottom of the sea."

"Gee, thanks," said Poseidon.

"And what if you're wrong?" Zeus asked. "What if it turns out that the merpeople's tridents have no powers at all?"

Hera shrugged. "What if it turns out Oceanus's trident doesn't have any? I guess we'll find out who's right soon enough." She clutched the dolphin's dorsal fin with one hand and sent them a confident wave of farewell. Obviously she figured she was going to be right.

"Bye, then," said Zeus.

"Later," said Poseidon. "Lots of cluck—I mean *luck*."

Before the dolphin zipped off across the water, it looked up at Poseidon and winked.

"Whoa!" said Poseidon as it swam off. "Did you see that?"

Zeus nodded. "First the sea serpents, then the merpeople. And now the dolphin. For someone who's scared of the sea, you have an odd effect on its creatures."

"What did you see when those Sirens called to us?" Poseidon asked out of the blue.

"What did *you* see?" Zeus hedged, embarrassed to say.

Poseidon's eyes shifted away. He looked a little embarrassed too. "Nothing. It was dumb. Let's just go."

With the wind filling the ship's sails, they sped north. It was more peaceful now that Hera was gone. Zeus's ears enjoyed the quiet, but he kind of missed her.

Still, he was pretty sure he and Poseidon were on the right track. And that Hera was on the wrong one. After all, the arrow on his stone amulet had pointed steadily north all day. Chip wanted them to go that way.

As they sailed on, the sea grew even angrier,

rocking them from side to side. Huge bubbles broke the surface of the water as it roiled and boiled. The surf sizzled and splashed against the rocky shores of islands they passed. Shores with even more shipwrecks.

Zeus checked his amulet. The arrow had changed from black to red and was spinning around in circles. *Huh?*

"I think we're here," he said.

Poseidon looked around nervously. "So where's Oceanus?"

Without warning, a giant golden claw-hand rose from the sea. It lifted the *Stinker* above the water. Then it flung the boat away in a high arc.

One minute they were zooming through the air. The next, they were falling!

"Hang on!" Zeus yelled. Thinking fast, he grabbed the thunderbolt from his belt. If it fell into the sea, he and Poseidon could fry.

With all his strength Zeus hurled the bolt. "Fly to the closest island!" he commanded. Bolt zoomed off.

In the very next instant Zeus and Poseidon were dashed under the waves of an angry sea.

CHAPTER SIX

In Hot Water

"Zeus, where are you?" It was Poseidon's voice.

Treading deep underwater, Zeus could barely hear him. He looked up. Their ship was directly above him. It hadn't sunk! He kicked his feet and shot to the surface of the water. Poseidon was sitting on the boat, which was now floating upside down.

"Here I am," Zeus gasped. "And you didn't melt after all!"

"Yeah, well, I could've drowned, though," Poseidon said. Quickly he changed the subject. "Think that was Oceanus just now?"

"If it was, he's in a bad mood. Let's get to land," Zeus said, pointing toward the nearest island. "I have to find Bolt. And I think the boat might need repairs."

One of their oars came floating by, and he nabbed it. Then Poseidon reached out an arm and helped pull him from the water.

Sitting atop the overturned *Stinker*, Zeus rowed toward shore. The wild, boiling sea fought them all the way, tossing them about. At any moment they might sink.

"We're going nowhere fast," Poseidon said. He slid into the water behind the boat. With powerful kicks he propelled it forward faster than Zeus could even paddle.

"Thought you said you couldn't swim!" Zeus said in surprise.

"Guess I was wrong," Poseidon said, sounding surprised too.

They'd only gone a dozen yards when Zeus heard an odd clacking noise. Thinking he had water in his ears, he tilted his head to one side.

From behind him Poseidon asked, "Um, Zeus? Do you think that, besides his clawed hands, Oceanus has lots of muscles? And maybe a long beard?"

"How would I know?" asked Zeus. "I've never seen him. Unless he was in the forest with the other Titans the night I rescued you from King Cronus."

The clacking sound had grown louder.

Strange. Zeus tipped his head to the other side in case the water was in his other ear.

"I wonder if Oceanus also has horns on top of his head," Poseidon went on. "Horns that look like crab claws."

"Horns like crab claws?" Zeus laughed at the idea.

"WHAT'S SO FUNNY ABOUT CRAB CLAW HORNS?" boomed a voice.

Zeus whirled around so fast, he nearly toppled over. There, swimming beyond Poseidon, was a muscular, bearded giant. One with claw hands, who also had two big crab claws growing from the top of his head! The claws were all angrily clacking together.

"Oceanus?" Zeus squeaked the question.

"That's my name. Don't wear it out," the Titan declared. His skin was golden, and his long, thick serpentine tail floated behind him in a loose coil.

"Uh, okay," Zeus said.

"Well? State your business!" Oceanus commanded. *Clack, clack, clackety-clack!* went his claws, like he was just itching to pinch somebody.

Zeus wished Poseidon would speak up. Why should *he* have to do all the talking? He glanced toward the end of the boat, where Poseidon had been. He'd disappeared! That coward. Was he hiding under the boat?

"Well?" Oceanus prodded. He glided closer.

"Pythia sent us," Zeus explained, paddling faster. If he could get to the island and find Bolt, he'd have a weapon to use against this crazy claw guy. "She's this oracle in Delphi. And according to her prophecy—"

Oceanus frowned, his bushy green eyebrows forming a V. Slowly he rose from the sea until he rode the water with his tail.

"I'm supposed to find a magical trident," Zeus rushed on. "If you'd let me borrow yours, maybe I could use it to calm the sea, and—"

"WHAT?" The Titan's golden face turned purple with rage. "HOW DARE YOU! I made these seas furious—and furious they will stay."

Rearing back, he uncoiled his tail. It whipped toward Zeus, ready to lash him. Zeus ducked, sure he was a goner.

But before the Titan's tail could strike, Poseidon popped up in the water. Right between Oceanus and Zeus. Reaching up with one hand, Poseidon knocked the tail away. It seemed to cost him little more effort than swatting a fly.

Zeus stared in amazement. Oceanus's tail had to weigh a ton!

As Oceanus tried to right himself, Poseidon swam to Zeus. "I've seen it!" he exclaimed in hushed excitement.

"Seen what?" asked Zeus. He was still thinking about what had just happened. Did being in water somehow give Poseidon superstrength?

"The trident," Poseidon said. "He's got it strapped to his side like a sword. It's all gold and glittery. Way more magnificent than that merman's trident."

All too quickly Oceanus recovered from the shock of having his tail shoved aside by a puny Olympian. He gave chase, zooming smoothly through the water toward them. Since his back was to the Titan, Poseidon didn't notice.

"Watch out!" Zeus warned.

Poseidon whirled to face Oceanus. "Give me the trident, you overgrown snaky crustacean," the boy commanded. "It's mine!"

"Shh! Are you crazy?" Zeus hissed. "Oceanus will send us both to a watery grave! Besides, what makes you think the trident is meant for you?"

Before Poseidon could reply, Oceanus bellowed at them. "Overgrown snaky crustacean, am I?" *Whap!* His powerful tail uncoiled and smacked the water.

"Nyah, nyah. Missed me!" Poseidon yelled back. "You don't deserve that trident. You've been using it for evil instead of for good."

Suddenly Zeus caught on. Poseidon was trying to goad Oceanus into *using* his trident. Because until it was freed from his side, they had no hope of grabbing it away from him.

"Hey, Fishbreath!" Zeus called out to Oceanus. "I bet your trident is only a fake. I bet it doesn't have any powers at all. It's probably not even real gold!"

"Fake? I'll show you how *not* fake it is!" Oceanus roared. All at once the trident flashed golden in his fist. He pointed its three-pronged tip at the water. As he drew the trident upward, the water followed. It was like he'd raked the ocean into a towering wave!

Uh-oh, thought Zeus. But it was too late to take back his taunts.

Just before the wave crashed down, Zeus saw Poseidon dive beneath the water. Then the wave hit, and Zeus was lost in a swirling whirlpool.

CHAPTER SEVEN

On the Island

Luckily, the gigantic wave didn't do Zeus in. But it did wash him and the *Stinker* all the way to the shore of a nearby island.

Standing on the beach, he looked out to sea. Thunderation! Unfortunately, he couldn't see anything through the rising steam. He could hear Oceanus and Poseidon battling it out, though. *Splash!*

"Ow!"

"Take that!"

He wanted to be out there too! At the Delphi temple in Greece, Pythia had called him a hero in training. But a true hero would be in the sea right now, helping Poseidon fight Oceanus.

Zeus righted the boat. Then he pushed it back into the water and hopped in. *P.U.!* It stunk inside. Clumps of rotting seaweed had gotten twisted around its broken mast. "*Stinker*" really was a good name for the boat now.

Its sail was in rags, and its broken mast was useless. He started to paddle, but soon the boat began leaking. It had a hole in the bottom the size of his fist! No way would he make it without repairs. He turned around and dragged the *Stinker* back onto the beach.

Then he rushed inland to look for something to plug the hole. Up ahead in an outcropping of rock, he saw something sparking.

"Bolt! Is that you?" he called. The sparking grew brighter and more frantic. Running over, Zeus found the thunderbolt stuck in a boulder, tip first.

"Calm down," he soothed. He grabbed it with both hands and wrenched it out of the rock. It was easy—like pulling a knife from a block of cheese.

"If *I* can do this so easily, why couldn't you get loose on your own?" he wondered aloud. "For the same reason you couldn't get out of that cone-stone back in Pythia's temple? Maybe certain kinds of rock are like thunderbolt traps, huh?"

The thunderbolt didn't answer, of course. But once it was free, it darted here and there. It did flips and pinwheels in the air around him, glowing and sparking.

"Happy to see me?" Zeus asked, laughing.

He tugged his belt away from his waist, making a space. "Small!" he instructed. Instantly Bolt shrank to dagger size, dove for his belt, and slid under it. Then the thunderbolt went still.

Zeus got back to business, hunting for sap, reeds, and bits of wood. His thoughts were racing. Now that he had Bolt, he could use it to fight Oceanus. But though his aim was improving with every throw, he couldn't risk hurling Bolt over the water. He might electrocute every creature in the whole sea. Including Poseidon.

Swimming was out too. He wasn't that good at it. Not like Poseidon had turned out to be. No, his only hope was to fix the boat. And fast!

He ran back to the *Stinker* and flipped it over. Then he plugged the hole in its bottom with the stuff he'd collected.

Out at sea the battle raged on. *Clack-clack!*

Splash! "Ow!" Now and then Zeus caught flashes of the golden trident through the steam.

Minutes later the boat was ready. By rocking it back and forth, Zeus managed to turn it upright again.

Just as he launched, the entire sea quieted. The steam began to clear. Was the battle over? Where were Oceanus and Poseidon? Who had won?

Zeus paddled out in the boat, his heart pounding with worry. He gazed in all directions across the water. It was eerily calm and empty.

"Poseidon!" he called. No answer. His panic multiplied. What if Poseidon was dead?

But then, not more than twenty yards away, Poseidon's head popped up out of the water. Another head popped up too. It wasn't Oceanus's, though. It was another boy's.

Poseidon held the golden trident high in

triumph. Its glittery length flashed in the sunlight. "Yes! I beat him!"

Then he pushed the trident underwater. The two boys straddled its long handle. Suddenly they were zooming across the sea toward Zeus fifty times faster than he could paddle. *Whoa!*

Poseidon drew up beside the boat. "Zeus, meet Hades," he said, idling the trident just enough to keep it afloat. "Found him at the bottom of the sea. Oceanus was under orders from Cronus to keep Hades prisoner there."

The new boy shook the water from his dark, curly hair, then stared at Zeus. "I remember you. You're the one who freed us from Cronus's belly, right? Thanks for nothing," he said in a gloomy-sounding voice.

"Hey!" Zeus protested. "What's that supposed to mean?"

"It means I liked it in that belly," Hades

informed him. "It was better than being held captive undersea. It's cold down there!"

"Sorry," Zeus said, feeling kind of annoyed. Talk about ungrateful!

"Oceanus had Hades locked inside a big air bubble so he could breathe. He couldn't escape it without drowning," Poseidon explained. He did a few fancy zigzag turns on the trident. One hard turn sent a fan of water spraying over Zeus. "Oops. Sorry." Poseidon came to an abrupt stop.

"Watch it!" Zeus protested, brushing seawater from his eyes.

"Yeah. This trident is magic, you know," Hades warned Poseidon. "Be careful."

Poseidon just shrugged, acting cool. Winning a battle against a sea god had made him a little bit full of himself. Zeus couldn't blame him, though. It was a pretty epic victory.

"You wouldn't believe the great palace Oceanus

has got," Poseidon told Zeus. "It's way down deep. Tons of rooms. All carved out of coral. Shells and pearls everywhere. The guy is rich!" He was zooming around the boat in tight circles now.

Zeus stared at him, a little jealous. "You got all the way down to the bottom of the sea?" There was no way he could ever swim deep enough to see this fabulous palace. "How did you hold your breath for so long?"

"I don't know," said Poseidon. "It was like I didn't need to breathe. Weird, huh?"

I'll say, thought Zeus. Suddenly it all clicked together. Poseidon's not needing to breathe in water. His new strength and swimming ability. Fish giving themselves up whenever he was hungry. The way the sea serpents, merpeople, and that dolphin had stared at him.

The creatures of the sea had recognized Poseidon as their leader! The trident really was intended for him. Poseidon's hands were *the right hands.*

"Um, can we go? Oceanus is still down there," Hades said nervously. "Caught in his own net, thanks to Poseidon. But I doubt it'll hold him for long. We should scram, and quick."

Zeus shuddered at the thought of Oceanus escaping again. Those claws of his looked sharp. "Once he does get free, he'll come after his trident," Zeus said. "And *us*. I say we take him captive now, while we have the upper hand."

Hades went pale at the suggestion.

"No way! Are you bonkers?" asked Poseidon.

"He's a Titan, isn't he?" Zeus argued. "If he gets out of that net, he'll go right back to helping King Cronus again. Wouldn't it be smarter to find some kind of prison and take him there while he's tied up?"

Honestly, thought Zeus, *didn't they get it?*

The trident might be rightfully Poseidon's. And Poseidon could swim ten times better than him. But *Zeus* had ten times more *brains*.

"I don't want to be anywhere around him if he gets loose from that net," Hades warned. "One flip of his tail, and—" He drew a finger across his throat.

"Anyway, how would we carry him to a prison?" Poseidon added. "He's too big to fit in the boat or on the trident."

"Well, what do you guys suggest, then?" Zeus asked.

"Run!" yelled Hades. He was staring at something in the distance, his eyes wide.

Zeus shook his head. "That won't help." But then he stopped talking as he heard an all-too-familiar sound.

Clackety-clack-clack!

CHAPTER EIGHT

Titan Transport

O ceanus was on the loose again! He was still mostly trapped in the net, but he'd poked his head and tail free. And now he was zooming toward them, muscles bulging and claws clacking.

Poseidon spun the trident so Zeus could climb onto the end of its handle behind Hades. "Hurry! Get on!"

Once all three boys were atop the trident,

Poseidon cut across the water. Instead of fleeing, though, he headed straight for Oceanus!

"Turn! Turn!" Zeus and Hades begged.

Poseidon ignored them. They got closer and closer to the Titan. It looked like they were going to ram him!

At the last minute Zeus ripped the thunderbolt from his belt and tossed it high. "Hover!" he commanded, hoping it would obey.

Fearing for their lives, he and Hades both jumped off the trident. *Splash! Splash!*

As Zeus watched Poseidon ride onward, he saw that Oceanus had slowed his approach. The Titan began to back away. Something had scared him. Was it Poseidon? Suddenly Oceanus turned tail and dove, making a break for it.

Poseidon leaped from the trident, still clutching it in one fist. As his feet hit the water, they turned scaly. So did his legs. He'd sprouted a fish tail! "Wa-hoo!" he shouted. "Is this the coolest, or what?"

He slapped the surface of the water with his new tail. He twirled the tip of it overhead. Slick rainbow-colored scales glittered in the sunlight.

Zeus and Hades swam in closer. "Awesome tail!" Hades called out.

"Admire it later!" Zeus hollered. "What about Oceanus?"

"Chill out," Poseidon said. "I'm going fishing. I'll snag that Titan in no time. Just watch me." Balancing his new tail on the surface of the water, he poked the three-pronged end of the trident into the sea. In the exact spot where Oceanus had disappeared.

"Long!" he commanded. Instantly the trident began to lengthen in the water. It extended deeper and deeper. It could change size like Bolt! Speaking of Bolt, Zeus looked up. The thunderbolt had obeyed him and was hovering high overhead. *Phew.*

Poseidon began raking the trident back and forth. Minutes later he smiled big. "Gotcha!"

As Poseidon reeled Oceanus in, Zeus and Hades treaded water nearby. By the time the Titan reached the surface, the trident's handle had shortened itself again.

Oceanus glowered at the boys as he tried to wriggle loose from the net. But though his head and tail were free, his arms and torso were still tangled in it. The net was made of tough stuff. Though Oceanus tried to cut through it with his claws, he couldn't do it. "RELEASE ME AT ONCE!" he demanded.

"Not gonna happen," said Poseidon. He sprang from the sea and landed on Oceanus's back. The instant Poseidon left the water, his tail turned back into legs. He scrambled upward, scaling the sturdy net.

The Titan twisted around. His claws reached for Poseidon, trying to pinch him through the net. But Poseidon dodged them. When he reached Oceanus's shoulder, he touched the sharp tips of the trident to the back of Oceanus's neck. "You're *our* prisoner now."

The claws went still. Oceanus turned his head, glancing fearfully at the trident. Whatever magic powers it had, he seemed scared of them. Of course, he would know just how powerful the trident was!

"C'mon!" Poseidon called to Zeus and Hades. The boys swam closer and grabbed on to the net. They climbed higher up Oceanus's back until they were alongside Poseidon. Now far above the water, Zeus summoned Bolt with a wave of his hand. Instantly the thunderbolt zoomed down and slid back under his belt.

"Onward!" Poseidon commanded Oceanus. "Take us to—um, land. Back to the dock we started from."

"You want me to give you a ride?" Oceanus laughed slyly. "Be glad to. But first you'll have to free me from this net."

"No way. How dumb do you think we are?" Hades shot back.

Oceanus pretended to think. "Well, on a scale of dumbness from one to ten, I'd say— Ow!"

Poseidon had interrupted him with a nudge from the sharp end of the golden trident. "Get moving!" he told the Titan.

Zeus could hardly believe it when Oceanus obeyed. But then again, the Titan didn't have much choice. Now that the magical trident was in Poseidon's hands, he was quickly learning how to use it.

The wind whistled in the boys' ears as Oceanus plowed across the sea toward Greece. They were moving faster than the seagulls flying overhead!

"What'll we do with him after we're back in Greece?" Hades shouted over the roar of the wind. "He'll be a danger to all Olympians if we let him go free."

"You got that right," Oceanus agreed before Zeus could reply.

"Stop listening!" Poseidon commanded. The boys huddled closer together, talking more quietly so the Titan wouldn't hear.

"We have to keep him tied up in this net," Zeus told his companions. "Until we can imprison him."

"But where'll we find a prison strong enough to hold him?" asked Hades.

Zeus's amulet twitched against his chest.

He jerked in surprise, almost losing his grip on the net.

"Ake-tip itan-Tip oo-tip artarus-Tip," the chip squeaked in its tiny voice.

Hades's dark eyes widened in surprise.

"Take Titan to Tartarus," Poseidon translated slowly. "Where's that?"

Zeus shrugged. "No clue." As Poseidon explained about Chip to Hades, Zeus lifted the amulet. He watched its black symbols rearrange themselves into squiggly lines and arrows.

"A map!" he said at last. "It must be showing us the route to Tartarus. And the dock's on the way."

The boys traveled on, following the map and giving Oceanus directions. They kept an eye out for Hera but didn't see her on land or sea. Zeus figured she'd be waiting for them. But when they reached the dock, she wasn't there.

"Do you think King Cronus captured her again?" Poseidon asked anxiously.

"I didn't know you cared," teased Zeus. But the thought that Cronus or his Cronies might've nabbed her had him worried too.

"Just because I fight with her doesn't mean I want her to get recaptured," said Poseidon. He and Hera bickered a lot, but they *did* care about each other, Zeus realized. They'd grown up together and were both Olympians, after all. Whatever that meant.

"I vote we keep going," said Hades. "We can come back and search for her later."

"He's right," said Zeus. "We have to get Oceanus locked up. For everyone's safety. Including Hera's."

Once they were on land, Oceanus shed his serpent's tail for a pair of legs so that he could walk. "Where are you taking me?" he demanded.

"That's for us to know and for you to . . . uh . . . not know," said Poseidon. "Just march." He prodded Oceanus with the trident.

"Hey, watch it with that thing," the Titan complained. But he picked up his pace.

The boys continued to ride on his back, clinging to the net that covered his torso. Zeus checked the amulet now and then, making sure they stayed on course.

At the top of a winding road, they began to drop down through a thick forest. Eventually the forest gave way to an open valley.

"We should have waited for Hera," said Poseidon.

Zeus wondered if he was right. What if their decision to go on without Hera had been a bad one? On the other hand, she might never have shown up. He really hoped she was okay. Even if she did think he was one of Cronus's spies!

With that on his mind he turned toward Poseidon. "We have the trident now. So what was the big secret she was going to tell me once we got it?"

Poseidon shrugged. "I promised not to say. You'll have to ask her. If we ever see her again, that is."

"Hush," Hades hissed. With a finger to his lips he nodded across the valley to the hills on the other side. "Something's moving up there."

Overhearing, Oceanus halted. "He's right."

"Where?" asked Poseidon, shading his eyes.

Hades pointed, and Zeus's eyes followed his finger. Seconds later they all saw someone— or some*thing*—dart from behind a rock to the cover of a tree.

"Cronies?" Poseidon wondered aloud. He squinted at the place where the figure had been.

"Unfortunately, not," grumped Oceanus, who actually *liked* Cronies. "They wear armor."

"Then, what?" Zeus asked. The figure had moved so quickly, he hadn't had time to see it clearly. He was about to suggest they find a place to hide, just in case, when bloodcurdling yells filled the air.

"YAAAH!" All at once the hillside came alive with dozens of strange creatures. Strange because they had no heads. Instead their faces were smack in the middle of their chests!

Oceanus's eyes widened. "Cronus has let loose the first of the Creatures of Chaos! We're doomed!" His voice was a horrified wail.

"Creatures of Chaos?" Zeus echoed. "I remember that the king was talking about unleashing them, when I overheard him at his meeting in the forest with the other Titans." And Pythia had mentioned them in her prophecy. Hadn't she said the trident could defeat them?

"Don't you get it?" bellowed Oceanus.

"Those are Androphagoi coming at us. They're monsters! Man-eaters!" He shuddered. "They'll eat us alive!"

"YAAAH!" screamed the mouths in the middle of the monsters' chests. They had long, sharp teeth. Bone-crunching teeth! Brandishing clubs and spears, the beasts streamed downhill to the valley like big ants from an enormous anthill.

"It's an ambush!" shrieked Poseidon.

CHAPTER NINE

The Androphagoi

Oceanus turned and ran back the way they'd come. No need to prod him with the trident to get him to move this time!

Soon they were back in the forest. The Androphagoi were gaining on them. Zeus and Poseidon had weapons, of course. But would Poseidon's trident and Bolt really be a match against an entire army of monsters? Zeus had his doubts, despite the oracle's words.

As Oceanus passed a tree, Zeus leaped from his back, grabbing on to a limb. "Spread out and climb!" he called to the others. "We can pick them off one by one from high in the trees."

One of the monsters blew a dart. It zoomed past Zeus's shoulder as he scrambled up the tree trunk.

Poseidon and Hades followed his lead, also leaping onto trees. But Oceanus was much too big and heavy for any tree to hold him. And he couldn't have climbed very easily while wrapped in his net, anyway.

"Hide somewhere. But don't try to escape," Poseidon warned him.

Pulling Bolt from his belt, Zeus shouted "Large!" Sparking and sizzling with electricity, the zigzag bolt lengthened in midair.

"After them!" he commanded. "The Andro-phagoi, I mean," he added quickly.

Bolt flew toward the ground, then zipped through the forest. Soon high-pitched yips and unearthly grunts rang out as the thunderbolt struck one monster after another. Once they'd been zapped, the Androphagoi vanished into thin air. *Pop! Pop! Pop!*

They must be under some kind of enchantment, Zeus realized. Unfortunately, the remaining monsters didn't retreat. They just kept coming, one after another.

In a nearby tree Poseidon extended his trident downward. He speared the Androphagoi as they ran by. The trident's prongs flashed golden as they jabbed the beasts in their behinds. *Pop! Pop! Pop!* The creatures burst like bubbles.

But their numbers were huge and they continued to swarm through the forest. Things were looking bad.

Whack! Something shook the tree Zeus was

in. His foot slipped. He had to grab at a branch to keep from falling.

When he looked down, he saw one of the headless monsters on the ground directly below him. "YAAAH!" The face on its chest grinned up at him. Its jaws were slobbering. It swung its club again. *Whack!*

The tree trembled, but Zeus held on tight. The monster kept whacking, but the tree didn't fall. *Good thing the Androphagoi don't have saws,* Zeus thought. But, unfortunately, they did have legs. Abandoning his club, the monster below began to climb.

"Back off!" yelled Zeus. He went higher. But the Androphagos didn't give up. Putting two fingers to his lips, Zeus gave a loud whistle. "Here, Bolt. Come here, boy!" he called frantically.

Zeus could see the thunderbolt flashing here and there at the edge of the forest as it popped other monsters. But it must not have heard him. Looked like it was up to Zeus to save himself this time.

The monster was close now. Its razor-sharp teeth gleamed as it opened its mouth wide. "YAAAH!" it yelled. The Androphagoi sure did have a limited vocabulary.

By now Zeus had climbed to the top of the tree. There was no place to go except down. If he jumped, he'd only break his legs. Then he'd be boy meat for sure!

He felt hot breath on his ankle. The Androphagos snapped its jaws, trying to bite him. Why did practically everyone he'd met since leaving his cave in Crete want to eat him? Zeus wondered.

Sharp teeth clamped around the heel of his sandal. As the creature tugged on it, Zeus tried to kick it off. He lost his balance. His arms flailed in midair. Suddenly he and the monster were both falling.

Whump! The Androphagos landed on the ground on its back. *Thump!* Zeus landed on top of it. The monster had cushioned his fall!

Pop! It vanished, leaving Zeus sprawled on the ground alone.

Just then Bolt zoomed back. Zeus leaped up and brushed himself off. Bolt hovered in front of him. "About time you got here," he scolded. "I was almost mincemeat."

Bolt's glow dimmed. It stopped sparking. Zeus sighed. "Sorry. That wasn't fair. I know you were busy."

Looking around, he realized that the Androphagoi were completely gone. All of them. *Vanished.*

He smiled. "Good work, Bolt." At his praise the thunderbolt glowed brightly again. Making itself as small as a dagger, it slid under the belt at Zeus's waist.

Zeus gave it a little pat. "You're better than any old golden trident," he murmured. "I'll miss you when you go back to that Goose guy."

"We defeated them!" he called out to the others. Hades and Poseidon climbed down from their trees and joined him.

Having helped defeat the Androphagoi, Poseidon's trident now glowed with pride. It seemed as happy to be in Poseidon's possession as Bolt was in Zeus's.

The difference was that the trident really did belong to Poseidon now. Or so it seemed. The thunderbolt was only on loan to Zeus till Goose turned up to claim it.

"Wait! Where's Oceanus?" Poseidon asked, looking around.

Zeus had half-expected the Titan to slip away

while the battle raged. But they found him caught on a thorny branch, tangled up in his net.

After scrambling onto Oceanus's back, Poseidon used the sharp tips of the trident to cut Oceanus loose from the thorns. Zeus helped, using the thunderbolt to burn through the net's fibers.

"Cut my arms free while you're at it," Oceanus commanded in a sugary-sweet voice. "My claws are useless on it. I promise I won't try to escape."

"Don't believe him," Hades said, glancing at the Titan's clawed hands. "He's crossing his claws."

Poseidon glowered at Oceanus. "Swear on the trident."

The Titan glanced warily between Poseidon and the trident. Then he uncrossed his claws. "FINE!" he snarled, rolling his eyes. "I swear I won't escape." But no one noticed he was now crossing the claws on top of his head.

When they finished their work, the Titan's arms were free. The rest of the net still draped him like a cape, though. The boys clung to it as Oceanus began walking down into the valley again. They were all quiet for a time, just relieved to be alive.

"I never thought I'd say this about a fellow Titan," Oceanus muttered. "But it seems Cronus can't be trusted."

"We knew that a long time ago," muttered Zeus. "You just now figured it out?"

"Yeah, you've been following his orders!" Poseidon exclaimed.

"Like keeping me captive," Hades added.

"I had my reasons," Oceanus told them. "For one thing, Cronus is my king. I owe him allegiance. Besides, he told me you were plotting to overthrow him."

They were walking through a meadow now.

It was dotted with clumps of purple crocuses and other flowers. Ahead was a rocky hill they'd soon have to climb.

"Me?" said Hades. "I don't know how to overthrow anybody."

"Yeah, me either," said Poseidon. One of his arms was hooked through the net. With his free hand he twirled the golden trident like a baton.

Oceanus winced when Poseidon tossed the trident up into the air and almost missed it on the way down. "Careful! If you drop my trident, I'll—"

Poseidon's turquoise eyes flashed. "It's not yours now. It never really was. You stole it, didn't you!"

Zeus's ears pricked up. Was this true? How could Poseidon know that?

"Did not," Oceanus protested. "Cronus gave it to me years ago!"

"But he shouldn't have," Poseidon insisted. "It's mine." He glanced at Zeus. "When the sirens sang to us, I saw a vision of myself as a baby playing with this very trident. But it wasn't until I held it again that I knew it was truly mine."

Aha! thought Zeus. That explained Oceanus's wary glances at Poseidon. The Titan had known all along that the trident belonged to Poseidon!

"Did Cronus threaten to take back the trident if you didn't imprison me?" Hades guessed suddenly.

They'd reached the base of the hill. As Oceanus started to climb, he hung his head, then nodded. "To tell you the truth, he's always been sort of a bad apple. When we were young, he'd lie to get me in trouble. Just for fun." He clacked his crab claw hands. "He was always telling our parents I pinched him."

The three boys stared at the Titan in surprise. "Your parents?" Zeus said. "Does that mean you're—"

Oceanus nodded. "Brothers. Cronus is my *little* brother, to be exact." He paused before adding, "My *spoiled, bratty* little brother."

Whoa, thought Zeus. He'd often wished he had brothers and sisters, in addition to parents. But maybe being an "only" wasn't so bad!

Oceanus went on. "And now that he's unleashed the Creatures of Chaos, we're all doomed. Mortals and gods alike. He wants to rule over everyone. And Olympians are the only threat to his plan."

"Why are they a threat?" Zeus knew Hera and Poseidon suspected it had to do with magical powers. But maybe there was more to it than that.

"Because of the prophecy," Oceanus replied.

"What prophecy?" Zeus asked.

"The prophecy that an Olympian will rise up and lead other Olympians to defeat Cronus," Oceanus explained.

Before Zeus could get his mind around that, the ground below them began to rumble and shake.

"What now?" he wondered aloud.

CHAPTER TEN

The Oracle

Quickly the boys slid from the net to the ground. Zeus looked around wildly. Were more Androphagoi coming? Or an army of Cronies? Fortunately, he saw neither. He and the others jumped back in surprise as the earth split open in front of them.

"Pythia!" Zeus exclaimed as a cloud of glittery mist appeared. His companions gaped at her. It probably wasn't every day that they saw

magic this powerful. The boys were so intent on the oracle that they didn't notice when Oceanus began backing away.

The oracle's face, framed by long black hair, glowed within the mist. It was hard to see her eyes, though. Her glasses were fogged over as usual.

"Congratulations." The oracle smiled at the three boys. "The trident is now in the right hands—"

"Yes!" interrupted Poseidon. He pumped the trident up and down. "I knew it was mine!"

"Shh," said Zeus. "Let her finish."

"—and if used wisely, it will bring untold power, honor, and glory to the true god of the sea." She paused here, turning her foggy gaze on Poseidon.

"Stupefying starfish," he murmured in shock. "I'm the god of the sea!"

Well, that explains a lot, thought Zeus. Including why Oceanus seemed so afraid of Poseidon. It wasn't just to do with the trident. If Poseidon was god of the sea, then Oceanus was *beneath* him in rank.

"You have also defeated the first of the king's Creatures of Chaos," the oracle went on. Her gaze moved back to Zeus. "Well done. But your quest is not yet ended."

Excitement rose in Zeus at the possibility of more adventure. He leaned forward, listening intently. So did Poseidon and Hades.

"Next you must find the Helm of Darkness," Pythia informed them. "It rightfully belongs to the one who is lord of the Underworld. Find it and you will also find more of the persons you seek. Only, beware of the second of the king's Creatures of Chaos. For they are far more dangerous than the Androphagoi."

The second she stopped speaking, the mist vanished. So did she.

"Wait!" Zeus called out. "What's a Helm of Darkness? Who's the lord of the Underworld?"

But Pythia was long gone. Even the crack in the earth through which she'd appeared had vanished.

Hades frowned, mumbling worriedly. "More Creatures of Chaos? I don't like the sound of that."

"Me neither," said Poseidon. Then he looked around. "Hey! Oceanus is gone!" While their attention had been on the oracle, none of them had noticed the Titan slip away. *So much for promises. Maybe no Titan could be trusted!* thought Zeus.

As tall as Oceanus was, they still couldn't spot him anywhere. So they climbed to the top of the hill and gazed out across the valley. The Titan was nowhere to be seen.

"So much for trusting his word," said Hades. "I guess he's escaped."

"Do you think he heard Pythia?" Poseidon wondered. "Will he tell the king what she said?"

"I hope not. But there's no reason to go to Tartarus now," said Zeus. "Let's head for the Underworld instead. *Fast.* Before those half-giant Cronies can beat us there. Because if the Helm of Darkness belongs to the lord the Underworld, that's probably where we'll find it."

He checked Chip, figuring it would chart a new course. "Funny. It's still pointing the same way as before." He thumped it. No change.

Hades looked over his shoulder at the chip. "Maybe Tartarus is near the Underworld."

Zeus peered in the direction the arrow wanted them to go. In the distance he made out a huge marsh. A muddy, brown river snaked through it.

"All I know for sure is that we should head for that river," he said, pointing.

"Looks gloomy," said Poseidon. "And I bet it smells bad too."

Hades's face lit up. "Sounds perfect."

"Huh?" Zeus asked in surprise.

"He likes gloomy and stinky," Poseidon explained. "Like the inside of the king's belly."

Hades smiled dreamily. "Yeah."

What a weirdo, thought Zeus. He wondered what the other Olympians he hadn't yet met were like. And that made him think about Hera again. If all the Olympians were gods, then she'd be a goddess.

But goddess of *what*? Of being annoying, maybe?

That thought made him smile. She could be a pain at times. Still, he hoped she hadn't been eaten by the Androphagoi before they'd popped them all. Why, oh why, hadn't she waited for them like she'd said she would? Where was she now?

He should've asked Pythia when he'd had the chance. Not that she would've given him a straight answer. Oracles rarely did. But the next time Pythia appeared, he was going to get more out of her. Including why she was sending them on all these quests!

Still, crazy as it seemed, he looked forward to this new one. And one day soon perhaps all would be revealed.

Feeling destiny beckon, he started downhill toward the distant, gloomy river. "Follow me," he called to the other boys. And with that, they embarked on their next quest, heading for the Underworld. Together they would face whatever surprises and dangers awaited them there.

Hades and the
Helm of Darkness

For Ward Williams, best son ever —S. W.
For Paul, best brother ever —J. H.

Greetings, Mortal Readers,

I am Pythia, the Oracle of Delphi, in Greece. I have the power to see the future. Hear my prophecy:

Ahead I see dancers lurking. Wait—make that *danger* lurking. (The future can be blurry, especially when my eyeglasses are foggy.)

Anyhoo, beware! Titan giants now rule all of Earth's domains—oceans, mountains, forests, and the depths of the Underwear. Oops—make that *Underworld*. Led by King Cronus, they are out to destroy us all!

Yet I foresee hope. A band of rightful rulers called Olympians will arise. Though their size and youth are no match for the Titans, they will be giant in heart, mind, and spirit. They await their leader—a very special yet clueless boy. One who is destined to become king of the gods and ruler of the heavens.

If he is brave enough.

And if he can get his friends to work together. And if they can learn to use their new amazing flowers—um, amazing *powers*—in time to save the world!

CHAPTER ONE

Stinky River Styx

Zeus, Poseidon, and Hades stood on a hill, gazing downward. A river wound like a snake through the gloomy valley below. It was all that stood between them and their goal—the Underworld.

Zeus sniffed the air, then wrinkled his nose. "P.U.! What is that stinky smell?"

Poseidon pointed toward the valley with the

three-pronged end of his trident. "I think it's that river."

The river looked brown and sludgy. There was a giant sign by it that read: RIVER STYX.

Maybe the sign was written wrong, thought Zeus. Maybe it should really say: RIVER *STINKS*!

Hades gazed happily at the river. "What are you guys talking about? I think it's awesome!"

"You would, weirdo," said Poseidon. "Well, you know what I think? I think there's no way I'm going near that river. I think that oracle is crazy."

Zeus knew he meant Pythia, the Oracle of Delphi. She'd sent them here to the Underworld on a quest. They were supposed to find the Helm of Darkness. Whatever that was. As usual, she hadn't fully explained. She always seemed to expect them to figure these things out on their own.

"But you like water, remember?" Zeus told Poseidon. He tried to sound more cheerful and encouraging than he felt. "I mean, you're an Olympian—the god of the sea!"

They'd discovered this on their last quest to the Aegean Sea. There they'd found Poseidon's trident in the possession of a Titan named Oceanus. The trident was like a pitchfork, only cooler. They'd found Hades in the sea too.

However, they'd also lost Hera. She'd gone looking for the trident on her own. Who knew where she was now? Zeus hoped she was somewhere safe.

"I like clean, blue rivers," Poseidon informed him. "Not stinky gloppy skunk water. Besides, it's not just the river that creeps me out. It's that whole place down there. It's so—"

Honk!

The boys looked around in alarm. Where

that loud, deep honking sound coming
om? Right then a sudden spurt of hot steam
sprayed up out of the ground under Poseidon.
He jumped a foot high.

"Steamin' undershorts!" he yelled, grabbing
his behind with his free hand.

Honk! Psst! Another squirt of hot steam burst
unexpectedly from the ground. This one struck
Hades. *"Yeowch!"* He grabbed his behind and
hopped around too.

Honk! Psst! Honk! Psst! More spurts gushed
out of the ground.

Then one struck Zeus. He jumped in surprise
and pain. "Thunderation, that's hot!"

"Let's get out of here!" Poseidon called. The
boys ran toward the river.

Anytime they slowed, a honk sounded and
another spurt of steam attacked. *Honk! Psst!*
"Ow!" *Honk! Psst!* "Ow!"

"Last ferryboat to the Underworld!" shouted a voice up ahead. Zeus squinted his eyes at the boat. It was sailing toward them from the opposite side of the river. Since it was the same brownish color as the water, it blended in. That's why they hadn't noticed it before.

"A boat to the Underworld?" called Hades. "Perfect! Let's get on it."

"Like we have any choice?" Poseidon yelled back.

"Yeah," Zeus agreed breathlessly. "It's like we're being herded down to the boat." The spurts were chasing them, so they could only move forward.

And it wasn't just the three boys who were being rounded up. Dozens of other people began to appear. They streamed down the hill running for the boat too. Most of them were really old. But they were moving pretty fast.

As the boys got closer to the boat, they saw a man on board. He reached up to pull a string attached to a horn. Another loud honk sounded. More hot spurts shot out of the ground around them.

"Hey! I think that ferryboat horn is what's causing the steam to honk out," Zeus told his friends.

The three boys dashed the rest of the way to the ferry. Just as they were about to leap onto it, a hand blocked their way.

"Halt!" It was the man who had sounded the horn. He was pale, with long white hair and wrinkled skin. And he was wearing a hat with his name: Captain Charon.

He peered at them closely. "Are you dead?" he asked them.

Zeus nodded, breathing hard. "That's for sure. Dead tired. We could use a ride."

"No, I think he means—" Hades started to tell Zeus.

"All righty, then. Pay your fare," the captain interrupted. "Passage across the River Styx costs one obol. Each." He held out his hand, palm upward, waiting.

"Better pay the fee," a woman behind them advised. "It's either that or wander these shores for one hundred years."

"We don't have any money," Zeus admitted.

"Next!" said Charon, pushing the three boys aside. He let a man come forward. The man opened his mouth and stuck out his tongue. There was a silver coin on the tip of it!

Charon took the coin and flipped it high with his thumb. It arced through the air. *Plunk!* It landed in a coin bag tied at his waist.

"Get lost," Charon barked at the boys when they didn't leave. "You're blocking others who can cough up the fare. They're *dying* to get in."

Zeus and Poseidon just stared at him.

The ferryboat captain grinned. "That was a joke. Get it?"

"No," Zeus and Poseidon said at the same time.

But Hades burst out laughing.

Zeus and Poseidon looked at each other, not getting what was so funny.

"Finally," Charon said to Hades, sounding flattered. "Someone who appreciates a good joke. Are you with them?" he asked Hades, hooking his thumb toward Zeus and Poseidon.

Hades nodded.

"Okay, then. Just this once I'll overlook the fare. Welcome aboard!" Captain Charon stepped aside and waved the three boys onto his boat.

CHAPTER TWO

Wild Ride

Charon used a long pole to push the ferry-boat off the riverbank once everyone was aboard. As they began the trip back across the river, he smiled big.

"All righty, shades, you paid your obol. Now it's showtime!" he announced. "Let's see if I can bring a little *life* to this party!"

"Why is he calling everybody shades?" Zeus mumbled.

"Because that's what we are. Shadows of our former selves," explained the man standing next to him.

The boys stared at him, unsure what he meant. The others on board did look kind of pale, thought Zeus. But they were people, not shadows.

Just then Charon's voice boomed out, making everyone jump. "First a little humor. Who can tell me what the favorite game in the Underworld is?"

Before anyone could guess, Charon answered his question himself: "Pick-Up-Styx! Ha-ha-ha!"

The ship got dead quiet. Everyone looked confused.

Then Hades burst out laughing again. "Oh, I get it. You mean 'sticks,' which sounds like 'Styx.' Which is the name of this river. Ha-ha-ha! Good one!"

"Thanks. I got a million of 'em!" Encouraged,

Captain Charon proceeded to tell one joke after another. And he supplied all the punch lines himself without giving anyone a chance to guess them.

"What are the Greek gods' favorite musical instruments?" he asked. "Harp-ies."

"Why did the Greek student fail the test? Because he made too many mythtakes."

Zeus rolled his eyes. Poseidon groaned. Hades kept on laughing.

A man next to them leaned toward the boys. "Why did the shade beg the boat captain to stop telling lame jokes?" he asked. Then, just like Charon, he gave the punch line. "Because they were killing him—again."

Zeus looked at the man, still confused. Poseidon shrugged and said, "Whatever. But if his jokes don't kill us, the stink from this river probably will."

"I like Charon's jokes," Hades protested as the man turned away to talk to someone else. "And I still don't see what's wrong with the river."

The three boys looked over the railing. The muddy water below swirled with globby goop. Every now and then strange crocodiles with pink eyes surfaced to blink at them.

"It looks and smells like garbage stew," said Zeus.

"Yeah," Poseidon agreed. "Maybe I can clean it up with my trident, though. Like I fixed the sea on our last quest."

He stuck the tip of his gleaming golden trident into the mucky water. Then he stirred it around, chanting:

"Trident, trident—tried and true,
Turn this river sparkling blue."

After a few stirs the three boys gazed expectantly at the river. But it remained sludgy brown.

"Maybe your trident's powers don't work in the Underworld," said Hades.

Poseidon looked alarmed. "But they have to work! We can't go on a quest without magic. How will we defend ourselves?" He kept stirring and staring hopefully at the water. Nothing happened.

Now Zeus was worried too. He reached for his dagger-size thunderbolt and pulled it from his belt.

"Bolt! Large!" he commanded. But the zigzag bolt didn't sizzle or spark with electricity. And instead of expanding into a five-foot-long thunderbolt, it stayed the size of a small dagger.

Zeus and Poseidon shared panicky looks. Zeus had gotten used to having the thunderbolt's magic to help him out of bad situations.

He'd pulled the bolt from a magical stone in the temple of Delphi. Since then it had become a friend as well as an amazing weapon.

Friend? No! I shouldn't think of it like that, he thought. After all, the bolt didn't even belong to him. It belonged to some guy named Goose. The oracle had told him that. And as soon as Zeus found Goose, he was going to have to give him the bolt.

"Check your chip," Hades suggested. "See if it's working."

"Good idea." Zeus tugged on the leather cord around his neck. There was a smooth stone as big as his fist strung on the cord. He'd gotten it from the temple too. It was a magic amulet that could speak and give directions.

The three boys leaned in to study it.

"Chip?" Zeus asked it. But it didn't reply.

"No symbols," Poseidon noted. "No compass

arrow either. I think Hades is right. Our gadgets don't work here in the Underworld." He yanked at his trident. Its prongs had gotten tangled in some seaweed and wouldn't come loose.

"Which means we're doomed!" Hades moaned. Suddenly he didn't sound so cheery anymore. "We can't complete our quest without weapons or a compass to show us where to go. Remember what the oracle said?"

Zeus nodded, then quoted her from memory: "'You must find the Helm of Darkness. It rightfully belongs to the one who is lord of the Underworld. Find it and you will also find more of the persons you seek. Only, beware of the second of the king's Creatures of Chaos. For they are far more dangerous than—'"

Wham! Suddenly the ferryboat gave a hard jerk. Everyone on board stumbled and swayed. Zeus and Hades lost their balance and fell to their knees. Poseidon hung on to the railing with one hand and his trident with the other. Frightened cries sounded among the passengers.

Wham! The boat pitched forward again. "Those pink-eyed river creatures are snapping at my trident!" Poseidon shouted.

Each time the creatures missed, their flat, scaly noses hit against the boat's hull. That was what was causing the jerks.

"You—with the pitchfork!" yelled Captain Charon, pointing his river pole at Poseidon. "Don't tease the crockydeads!"

Three Rules

Wham! The boat shuddered yet again.

Chomp!

"Help! The crockydeads just sunk their teeth into my trident," Poseidon cried out in disbelief. "They're trying to steal it!"

Zeus jumped to his feet. He, Poseidon, and Hades all grabbed the trident's handle. They pulled hard. But the creatures were strong. They pulled back harder. It was a tug o' war!

Thump! The ferryboat bumped into the landing dock. They'd crossed the river and were on its far shore now. The jolt surprised the crockydeads into letting go of the trident. The three boys yanked it out of the river.

The crockydeads gave the boat one last slam with their snouts. Then they slithered away into the oozy brown water.

Captain Charon scowled at the three boys. "Troublemakers!" Using his ferryboat pole, he shoved them over to the gangplank. "Get off my boat!"

"Wait!" Zeus said. He grabbed the gangplank railing and stared at the captain. "Maybe this isn't the best time to ask, but my compass isn't working. I wonder if you could give us some directions before we go?"

"We're looking for the Helm of Darkness," added Poseidon.

Hades nodded hopefully. "Have you heard of it? We know it's here somewhere in the Underworld, but we don't know wh—"

Bam! Charon banged the end of his pole onto the deck, interrupting him. "There are three rules here in the Underworld."

He stepped toward them, wearing a fierce expression. Zeus, Poseidon, and Hades each took a step backward down the gangplank.

Charon held up a bony finger in front of their faces. "Rule number one: Don't ask nosy questions. Got it?"

The three boys nodded.

Charon took another step forward, and the boys each took another step backward. He held up two fingers. "Rule number two: Obey orders. Got it?"

The three boys nodded again.

"Good!" Charon gave them each another

sharp nudge with the long ferryboat pole. "Now get off this boat!"

"I wonder what rule number three is," Hades whispered to Zeus.

"Probably best not to ask," Zeus advised.

"Yeah, don't forget rule number one," said Poseidon.

The boys scuttled down the gangplank and hopped onshore. Other passengers swarmed past them in a hurry, sweeping them along. The ground was swampy and sucked at their sandals as they ran.

They were all heading for a fence a few dozen steps from the riverbank. It was made of iron spikes twice as tall as the boys. And it looked like it surrounded the entire Underworld!

Creeeak! Suddenly two giant gates in the middle of the fence magically swung open. Like the jaws of a giant sideways crockydead mouth, they looked ready to gobble everyone!

"Creepy," Poseidon muttered as they entered.

"You mean awesome!" Hades exclaimed.

"Why does this gate's magic work in the Underworld but ours doesn't?" Zeus wondered aloud. His companions were too busy studying their surroundings to answer.

"Look!" Poseidon said after they passed through the gates. He was pointing to something ahead. A magnificent golden throne! It was just sitting there in the middle of the swamp. Empty. Except for a square jeweled box that rested upon its velvet seat.

A big sign hung on the back of the throne. It read: BEWARE OF THREE-HEADED DRAGON DOG.

Hades had been pretty delighted with everything about the Underworld so far. But suddenly he screeched to a halt.

"Dog? Three-headed *dragon dog*?" His eyes

widened in fear. "I'm outta here!" He spun around and fled toward the gates and the riverbank.

"Come back! We need to stick together," Zeus called out. When Hades didn't stop running, Zeus and Poseidon chased after him.

The tall spiked iron gates were slowly swinging shut now that everyone was inside the fence. Beyond them the boys could see Charon angling his long pole against the shore of the River Styx. He pushed off.

"Wait for me!" Hades shouted to him. He put on a burst of speed, trying to make it through the gates in time.

CLANK! The gates swung shut in his face.

Hades grabbed on to two of the tall iron rails and stuck his face between them. "Take us with you!" he yelled toward the ferryboat.

Charon glanced back at the three boys. His ferry had already begun to cross the river toward the opposite shore. "No can do. Remember rule number three?"

The boys shook their heads. "No! You didn't tell it to us!" yelled Poseidon.

Charon shrugged. "Rule number three is: This ferry only carries passengers one way— *into* the Underworld. Once you're in, you're in. There's no escape."

Which meant they were all stuck in the Underworld—forever!

Grrr! Grrrowl! The three boys whipped around at the threatening sounds.

A snarling, drooly dog had appeared way behind them by the throne. The dog was scaly like a dragon and almost as big as the Delphi temple! It even had a dragon's tail that ended in a sharp arrowhead-shaped point. Besides that it had three heads! And each one was growling.

The three boys stood frozen at the sight.

"We're trapped!" wailed Hades.

"With no magic!" moaned Poseidon.

"C'mon," said Zeus. "We're sitting ducks out here by ourselves. Let's go mingle with the others before that dog notices us."

Quickly they made their way into the middle of the group. "We are *so* dead!" Hades muttered.

"True," said a man alongside him. "I was struck down in a battle a week ago." He drew a finger across his throat.

"I tripped over a bucket and broke my neck," said another man. "Kicked the bucket, you might say."

"Snakebite," said a third guy. "Never recovered."

"What are you guys talking about?" asked Zeus.

"How we bit the dust," the snakebite guy said matter-of-factly.

"You mean to say that you're all *dead*?" asked Poseidon. He'd finally put two and two together.

"Of course," said Hades. "That's what Captain Charon's jokes were about. Duh—didn't you get it?"

The others nearby in the crowd nodded.

Poseidon stared at Zeus and Hades, terrified. "*We're* not dead, though. Are we?"

"No way!" said Zeus, trying to calm him.

Then he had an awful thought. The oracle had promised they'd find *more of those they sought* here in the Underworld. Which meant more Olympians. But he'd also hoped it meant he might find his mom and dad—whom he couldn't even remember. His mom had left him in a cave in the care of a nymph, a goat, and a bee when he was just a baby.

But if everyone down here was already dead,

did that mean his parents were dead too? His heart sank.

Still, he tried to be brave for the sake of his two friends. "Don't worry. I didn't go to all that trouble to free you for us to end up dead!" he assured them.

Poseidon and Hades were two of the five Olympians he had rescued not long ago. They'd been trapped in the belly of Cronus, the big bad king of the Titans. With a toss of his thunderbolt down the king's throat, Zeus had made Cronus barf them all up. Now Zeus felt kind of responsible for them. At the end of this quest they just *had* to get out of here alive!

Except for a few growls now and then, it had gone quiet around them. The boys peeked from the crowd to see what was going on.

"That dog is herding everybody into three lines," said Poseidon.

There was a sign at the front of each line. Zeus squinted to read them all. "The sign on the left has a big *E* on it," he reported. "The middle sign has an *A*."

"The one on the right has a *T*," added Hades.

"E-A-T spells 'EAT'," said Poseidon.

Zeus cocked his head. "Eat?"

"I knew it!" wailed Hades. "That dragon dog is dividing us up into his breakfast, lunch, and dinner!"

CHAPTER FOUR

Thirsty

Hades' loud wail reached the dog's three sets of ears. Its three heads bobbed up. Its six red eyes narrowed, scanning the crowd.

"Looks like we're not so safe mingling with the crowd after all," said Zeus. "Let's get out of here."

"I'm with you," said Poseidon, peeling off from the line.

"Hey, wait for me!" called Hades. Ducking

behind some shades, the three boys tried to sneak off into the nearby bushes.

Woof! Woof! Woof!

"Oh, no!" yelped Hades. "He's spotted us!"

Sure enough the dragon dog came bounding over, all three heads snarling and drooling. In an instant the beast had the boys cornered.

Hades tried to run past it. But he tripped over a scaly log. The dog growled and leaned over him, baring three sets of teeth.

"Get away!" Hades shouted. Half-sitting on the log, he felt around for a weapon. His hand wrapped around something. A stake! Using both hands, he yanked it from the log. Maybe he could use it to defend himself.

Oww-ooo! The dog started howling. It tucked its tail between its front paws.

Suddenly the log was gone and Hades was sitting on the ground. He looked down at the

stake in his hand. It was actually a thorn. A very large thorn.

"Thunderation! You just pulled that thing out of the dragon dog's tail!" said Zeus.

"Tail?" echoed Hades. "I thought it was a log!"

"Run!" called Poseidon.

Before Hades could budge, the dog's heads whipped close. Three mouths opened, each showing two rows of icicle-sharp teeth.

Zeus gasped, sure that Hades was a goner.

Then the dog let out a gurgle that sounded sort of like, "Sir. Brr. Us." Its three tongues slipped out. *Lick! Lick! Lick!*

"Stop! Eew!" yelled Hades, swatting at the dog's heads. "Help! It's licking me to death!"

"No way I'm sticking around to be dragon dog dinner!" said Poseidon. Arms and legs pumping, he took off for the bushes.

Zeus grabbed Hades' arm and pulled him up. The two boys followed Poseidon.

"Is it after us?" Hades asked after they'd gone a dozen steps.

Zeus had been sure the dog would give chase. Glancing over his shoulder, he saw that it hadn't, though. In fact, it was just sitting there holding its tail and staring after Hades. It looked kind of sad, like its feelings were hurt.

Weird. But before Zeus could think much about it, he stumbled over a tree root. He slammed into his two companions. They all hit the ground. *Oof!*

Then all at once they were rolling down a hill, head over heels. When they finally came to a stop, they were in a valley. It was far below where they'd been only moments before. Far from that dog, thank goodness!

Poseidon's trident had wound up in Zeus's

lap. When Zeus sat up, the trident bumped the magical bolt tucked under his belt.

"Eware-bip the-Ip iver-Rip ethe-Lip," said a small, squeaky voice. It was Chip, Zeus's amulet! It spoke in Chip Latin, which was like Pig Latin, only you moved the first letter of each word to its end and added an "ip" sound in Chip Latin. Instead of the "ay" sound used in Pig Latin.

Poseidon looked over at Zeus, eyes wide. "Moldy mackerel! It's talking again?"

Excited, Zeus fished the amulet from the neck of his tunic and studied it. The symbols on it flickered briefly as he pushed the trident away. Then the amulet conked out again.

Disappointed, Zeus dropped the amulet back inside his tunic. "Guess not."

"But what did it say a minute ago?" asked

Poseidon. Zeus frowned uncertainly.

"Sounded like 'Beware the liver thief,'" said Hades.

"Well, that's a big help," said Poseidon. He picked up his trident, stood, and dusted himself off. Then he froze.

"You!" he blurted, staring at someone across the way. "Thanks for saving us the trouble of finding you again!"

Zeus and Hades scrambled to their feet to see who he was looking at.

Alongside a river that ran through the valley stood a familiar figure. A claw-handed Titan as tall as a tree.

"Oceanus," muttered Hades.

They'd captured Oceanus during their last quest, but he'd escaped before they could imprison him. Someday, somehow, they were going to have to lock all the Titan giants away.

Otherwise the Olympians would never be safe from them.

A woman with long dark red hair stood beside Oceanus. She, too, was as tall as a tree. Turning toward Oceanus, she gave him a metal bowl.

Grinning at the boys, Oceanus clacked one of his enormous claw hands at them in a taunting wave. Then, without a word, he dove into the river and swam away.

"Come back here, thief!" Poseidon shouted as the three boys rushed toward the river. He hadn't forgiven the Titan for stealing the trident from him long ago.

They'd all assumed that Oceanus had run off to King Cronus when he'd escaped them before. *Why did he come here instead?* Zeus wondered. *Who is this woman with him, and what are they up to?*

When the three boys reached the riverbank, they stared into the water where Oceanus had dived. This river was a clear, flowing blue. Very different from the River Styx. Zeus licked his lips, suddenly thirsty.

The red-haired woman still stood at the edge of the river. She seemed to be deep in thought. Suddenly she said, "I've got it! Roy G. Biv." She looked over at the boys. "What do you think?"

"About what?" Zeus looked up at her. And up, and up. "You're a Titan, aren't you?" he accused, before Poseidon or Hades could even open their mouths.

"Yes, I'm Mnemosyne," she replied, pronouncing it nuh-MAH-zuh-nee. "But fear not. I mean you no harm. Come, you boys look thirsty." It was like she'd read Zeus's mind!

She kneeled and dipped a tiny glass into the

river. In her fingers the glass looked as small as a thimble. When it was full, she held it out to the boys.

"Here, drink from my river," she told them. "Rest and forget your troubles awhile."

"Who's Roy G. Biv?" asked Poseidon. He stepped closer, reaching for the glass she offered. He took a drink.

"It's my new mnemonic," she explained easily. She pronounced the word as nuh-MAH-nick. "A mnemonic is a way of remembering something. For instance, 'Roy G. Biv' stands for the colors of a rainbow. Red, Orange, Yellow, Green, Blue, Indigo, Violet."

"Oh, I get it," said Hades.

Poseidon took another drink.

"My gift is the power of memory," she went on pleasantly. "That's how I came up with the idea for mnemonics like the one for the

rainbow. Down here the dead don't see many rainbows. I want to help them remember the colors."

Still kneeling, she dipped water from the river into two more glasses.

"We saw you talking to Oceanus," Zeus said. "What did he want?"

Mnemosyne shrugged, shifty-eyed. "Nothing much."

She smiled at Zeus and Hades. She held the two glasses of sparkling water out to them. "Drink," she crooned. "The waters of the River Lethe are the clearest of all five rivers in the Underworld. The most delicious, too. You'll forget any other water once you taste this."

Zeus was suspicious. But the sound of her voice and the sight of the water were making him thirstier than ever. He took the glass she offered. Beside him Hades took the other glass.

The River Lethe, thought Zeus. *Why does that ring a bell?* As he brought the glass to his lips, it clinked against his amulet. *That's it—the amulet!* he thought. *It had been trying to warn them about this river just a few minutes ago!*

He dropped his glass without drinking from it.

Thrusting out his hand, he slapped the glass from Hades' hands too, before he could drink.

Poseidon's glass was already half-empty. Still, Zeus leaped to Poseidon's side and swatted it away.

"Whoa! Why'd you do that?" Poseidon whined. "It was good."

"I just realized what Chip was trying to tell us before," exclaimed Zeus. "It said 'Beware the River Lethe'!"

Hades stepped back from the woman. "So you were trying to trick us!" he accused.

Mnemosyne laughed lightly and scooped two fresh glasses of water from the river. She tried to hand them to Zeus and Hades. "Don't be silly. Drink, Olympians," she ordered.

"What's an Olympian?" Poseidon asked blankly.

Zeus and Hades glanced at him in alarm.

"It's what, um, what *we* are!" Zeus told him. Mnemosyne didn't seem to realize that Zeus wasn't an Olympian like Poseidon and Hades. But that was probably a *good* thing.

She might fear him more if she didn't know he was only a mortal. Well, maybe he was a little more than a mortal. The oracle had called him a hero in training.

Looking determined, Mnemosyne rose to her feet. Zeus and Hades each grabbed one of Poseidon's arms. Then they skedaddled.

"Go ahead and run, little chicken boys!"

Mnemosyne yelled, not so nice anymore. "But if you think you'll escape us Titans this time— you can *forget* it!"

She let out a scary-sounding laugh. Then she dove into the river and swam away. Just as Oceanus had done.

CHAPTER FIVE

Forget It

Am I a farmer?" Poseidon asked.

"A what?" asked Hades, giving him a weird look.

"A farmer," Poseidon said, studying the sharp prongs of his trident. "If not, why am I carrying around this pitchfork?"

Zeus frowned. "That's your trident. You're god of the sea. Don't you remember?"

After they'd escaped Mnemosyne, they'd

wound up here, walking through a smelly sulfur field surrounded by hot lava. Poseidon had been asking dumb questions nonstop. Ever since he'd drunk from that river.

"Oh, yeah. I remember now," said Poseidon. "I also remember that you're Zeus." He looked over at Hades. "But who are you? And I know that this is my left foot. But what do you call my other foot?"

Zeus snapped his fingers. "Right—I've figured it out!"

He leaned over to Hades, speaking quietly. "Poseidon drank *half* the water in the glass Mnemosyne gave him, remember? It must've made him forget *half* of everything."

"Great. Just when we need our wits about us, he turns into a half-wit," Hades murmured back. "He's not going to be any help in finding the helm now. Not as long as he's forgetting stuff."

Just then Poseidon laid his trident on the ground so he could pull a rock out of his sandal. When he started walking again, he left his trident behind, forgetting all about it.

Hades sent Zeus a *See what I mean?* glance.

Zeus picked up the trident and held it under one arm. It bumped his bolt dagger with every step. Before he could return the trident to Poseidon, the amulet around his neck suddenly twitched.

Excited, Zeus pulled the amulet out of his tunic with his free hand. A single word appeared on its surface in bold black letters: UNDERWORLD. When it faded away, some small words appeared on the amulet. There were lines too, some straight and others wavy.

"It's a map!" Zeus exclaimed.

Hades and Poseidon came over to look. "Of what?" Poseidon asked.

"I think it's the Underworld," Hades told him.

Zeus peered intently at Chip's surface. There were three areas circled on the map. Each was labeled with a letter. One had a *T*. One had an *E*. One had an *A*.

Under the *T* was the word, "Tartarus." Under the *E* were the words "Elysian Fields." Under the *A* was "Asphodel Meadow."

"Tartarus," Zeus mused. He looked up at his companions. "That's where the amulet told us to imprison Oceanus, when we were on our last quest. Looks like it's a place right here in the Underworld."

"So if we can recapture Oceanus, we could still take him there," said Hades. "Mnemosyne, too."

Poseidon pointed to the map. He moved his fingertip from the *T* to the *E* and on to the *A*. "That spells 'TEA'!"

"Or if you rearrange the letters they could spell 'EAT'!" Hades exclaimed. "Like those signs we saw before by the Underworld gates."

"Hey! I bet 'EAT' was another one of Mnemosyne's mnemonics," said Zeus. "To help people remember the layout of the Underworld. *E* for 'Elysian Fields,' *A* for 'Asphodel Meadow,' and *T* for 'Tartarus.'"

"So that's why the dog was making the shades form three lines?" asked Hades.

Zeus nodded. "Yeah, those must be the three places where the dead go."

"Okay, so I guess the dog doesn't eat the dead after all," said Hades. "But what if he eats the *living*? Like us!"

Poseidon was looking confused. "Dog?" he asked. "We have a dog? Awesome!" He glanced around as if searching for it. "Here, poochie, poochie."

"I'll be glad when he gets his memory back," said Hades. "*If* he ever does."

"Ditto," Zeus agreed. He handed the trident back to Poseidon. "Here, you forgot something. Don't let go of it again." The instant he handed over the trident, the words and lines on his amulet blinked out.

"Oh, no!" said Hades.

"Don't worry. I memorized the map," said Zeus. "Elysian Fields is closest, so let's check it out first. It's this way."

On the way to the fields, they explained to Poseidon about the quest they were on. Ten minutes later they were standing in front of a tall green hedge. There was a door in it with a sign that read:

WELCOME TO THE ELYSIAN FIELDS

WHERE EVERYONE IS GOOD, AND DEAD

They pushed the door open and went inside. The fields were beautiful, with grapevines, fruit trees, gardens, and sparkling fountains. There was a fancy glass greenhouse at the far side of a field of wildflowers. The boys didn't see any people, though.

Zeus sniffed the sweet smell in the air. "Mmm. Roses."

Poseidon plucked a bunch of plump grapes from one of the grapevines. As they moved through the fruit trees, Zeus picked an apple and Hades picked a pear. They all began munching.

"So this is where the good people go after they die," said Zeus. "Nice."

"Yeah, I could get used to it," said Poseidon.

Hades shrugged. "I guess. I prefer the smell of sulfur swamp myself."

Zeus tossed his apple core away and reached

toward a tree for another apple. Suddenly he noticed a long golden strand of hair caught on a low branch. He recalled Hera's long, golden hair whipping in the wind when some half-giants had chased them during their last quest.

"This looks like Hera's hair," he said. Poseidon and Hades studied the golden strand too.

"You think when she went looking for the trident, she wound up here?" asked Poseidon.

It was weird, the stuff he could remember, when he forgot everything else. But at least he could remember Hera.

Suddenly they heard a girl's voice call out, "Help!"

Zeus gasped. "Was that Hera? Sounds like she's in trouble!"

"Hey! There's Oceanus," said Hades.

Sure enough, Oceanus was across the field of flowers now. It looked like he was locking the greenhouse. Was there someone imprisoned inside it. Hera, maybe?

Without thinking, Zeus whipped out his dagger-size thunderbolt. "Large!" he commanded. Nothing happened. The bolt didn't get big or spark with electricity. He'd forgotten it had no powers here in the Underworld. So why had Chip worked briefly before, he wondered.

"The three of us can take him," said Hades. "Even without magic."

"We have to try, anyway," said Poseidon.

Zeus tucked the bolt back into his belt. "Give us Hera!" he shouted to Oceanus.

"Make me!" Oceanus yelled back.

The three boys charged toward him across the field. They drew closer and closer. But right before they reached him, Oceanus disappeared into thin air!

CHAPTER SIX

The Helm

The minute Oceanus disappeared, Mnemosyne suddenly appeared a few feet away. She sprang into action. "Nyah, nyah. You can't catch me!" Her giant footsteps took her in another direction, away from the boys.

"They've got magic," said Zeus.

Poseidon nodded. "Magic that works in this world."

"Let's get her!" shouted Hades. The three boys rushed toward the orchard where Mnemosyne now stood.

Right before they reached her, she went invisible too! And then Oceanus reappeared. He ran over by the grapevines.

This appearing and disappearing happened over and over. Just when the boys thought they'd cornered one of the Titans, he or she vanished. Then the other Titan appeared nearby to tease and laugh at them.

When they charged Mnemosyne yet again, she was standing in front of a stone wall. Suddenly a bowl appeared in her hands. Quickly she put it on her head. Then she disappeared.

The boys couldn't stop in time. *Bam!* They crashed into the wall.

"Ow!"

"Ow!"

"Ow!"

Zeus sat up, rubbing the lump he'd gotten when his head hit the wall. "What's going on here? Why do we only see one of them at a time?"

"They must have something magic that's making them invisible," said Poseidon. "Maybe it's that metal bowl they keep passing between them."

"That's not a bowl," argued Hades. "It's a hat. Or a helmet. Why else would they keep putting it on top of their heads?"

"Wait! That's it!" said Zeus. "It's a helmet. As in '*helm*.' Get it?"

"That's right, fools!" said Mnemosyne. Though she was still invisible, she had obviously overheard them. "We are in possession of the Helm of Darkness." She laughed in that scary way again.

"Stole it from the throne of the lord of the Underworld himself!" Oceanus bragged. He was standing far across the field of wildflowers. It was as if he were afraid to come closer.

The boys huddled up to talk. "Why don't they attack us?" Zeus whispered.

"I think they're scared of your weapons," said Hades. "Of the magic in your bolt and Poseidon's trident."

"My trident is magic?" said Poseidon. He stared at it in awe.

Zeus rolled his eyes. He'd forgotten for a minute that Poseidon couldn't remember a lot of stuff. But maybe Hades was onto something.

"I bet you're right," Zeus told Hades. "I mean, that helm's magic seems to work fine in the Underworld. So maybe they haven't guessed that our magic *doesn't*."

"So let's pretend like it does work," Hades suggested.

"Yeah, maybe the Titans will fall for it," said Poseidon.

"Good plan," agreed Zeus. When they broke out of the huddle, he and Poseidon pulled out their weapons. They waved them menacingly over their heads.

Hades stood between them as they all confronted the Titans. "Give us the Helm of Darkness!" he commanded.

Oceanus eyed Poseidon's trident, turning pale. *Clackety-clack!* His claw hands clacked together nervously. He backed away. Then he ran to the far end of the hedge, leaped over it, and escaped.

"Wait for me!" shouted Mnemosyne. They couldn't see her, but they saw the tall flowers part in the field as she ran away. Seconds later they heard the two Titans arguing in the distance.

"It worked!" said Poseidon, punching his fist in the air. "They didn't guess that our weapons are temporarily powerless!"

"Help! Let me out of here," called a girl's muffled voice.

"Hera!" said Zeus. "She must be inside that greenhouse. C'mon. Let's rescue her."

"You and Poseidon can do that," said Hades. "I'll go after the helm." He turned toward the hedge.

Zeus grabbed his arm, stopping him. "No splitting up! That's how we lost Hera in the first place. I say we save her first. Then we'll all go after the helm together."

"Okay, fine," huffed Hades, sounding a little annoyed.

The three boys ran for the greenhouse.

Through its glass walls they could see that there was a girl inside. She was about their same age. But she wasn't Hera. There were flower blossoms in her light red hair, and she was wearing a flowing green dress.

"Who are you?" Zeus and Poseidon called through the glass to her at the same time.

"Demeter!" said Hades, grinning. He looked at Poseidon. "We grew up with her. All of us in King Cronus's belly. Then Zeus freed us. Remember?"

Poseidon shook his head. "Nuh-uh."

Hades reached for the greenhouse doorknob. "Ignore Poseidon," he called through the glass to Demeter. "He drank from the River Lethe. Lost half his memory."

"Oh, no!" she said, staring at them through the glass.

Poseidon looked a little embarrassed.

"It's locked," Hades announced when the

door wouldn't open. "Stand back, Demeter. We'll break the glass."

"You can't," Demeter told them. "Hera was imprisoned with me for a while, and we tried to break it. But it's magic. Unbreakable. So don't waste your time. Go after Hera." She made a shooing motion with her hand. "And then come back for me. She's in the Underworld too, trapped in Asphodel Meadow."

"Okay," said Hades. "We'll be back in a—"

"We'll set Demeter free first," Zeus insisted, cutting him off. "Then we'll search for Hera together."

Demeter smiled at him. "Hera told me you were a bossy thunderpants," she said teasingly.

Now it was Zeus's turn to look embarrassed. He hadn't minded when Hera had called him Thunderboy. But her other nicknames for him stunk worse than the River Styx!

"How'd you wind up here?" Zeus asked her, to change the subject. Meanwhile Poseidon began poking the lock with one of the sharp tips of his trident, trying to pick it.

"Mnemosyne brought me here on King Cronus's orders. She and Oceanus planned to take both Hera and me to a more secure hiding place today. To Tartarus." She shivered. "It's the lowest, foulest pit in the Underworld."

Just then the lock gave. Demeter shot out of the greenhouse door. "Come on," she called, making for the hedge. "To Asphodel Meadow!"

The four of them dashed through the hedge door and out of the Elysian Fields. Then Demeter stopped short, looking around. "Unfortunately, I don't know exactly where Asphodel Meadow is," she admitted.

"I do," said Zeus. "I saw a map." He took the lead, knowing it probably made him look bossy again. But sometimes the urge to take charge like this came over him. It was happening more and more as the days passed.

Ten minutes later the four of them came to a huge meadow of star-shaped white flowers.

"Wow! This must be what snow looks like," said Hades. Since the Olympians had been trapped in King Cronus's belly their whole lives, they'd never seen snow.

"It's asphodel," Demeter informed them. "The only flower that will grow in the Underworld outside of the Elysian Fields."

"Look—the Titans. They have Hera!" said Poseidon, gesturing across the meadow.

Sure enough, Oceanus and Mnemosyne were both visible now. Oceanus was carrying Hera. Mnemosyne was holding the helm.

"Hmm. That helm must only make you invisible if it's on your head," Zeus told the others.

Roarrr! Roarrr! Roarrr!

At the sudden sound the boys and Demeter whipped around in surprise. Behind them the enormous slobbering three-headed dog was headed their way, looking ready to pounce.

"Run for your lives!" yelled Hades. The four of them took off across the meadow, racing in different directions. The Titans laughed, apparently enjoying their fright.

The dog charged after Hades. Easily catching up, it frolicked around him in happy circles. Its three heads licked him, like Hades and the dog were long-lost best friends.

"Ick! Get away!" said Hades, swatting at the dog as he ran. Surprise—it didn't listen. "Fetch," he ordered desperately. He pointed toward the Titans.

Looking thrilled to have been given a job to do, the dog bounded across the meadow.

When it returned, it held Hera in one of its mouths.

There was also one Titan in each of its other mouths. Only a dog like this—one nearly as big as a temple—could manage such a feat!

All three captives were protesting loudly. The dragon dog dropped them at Hades' feet, like it was bringing him roadkill. The helm slipped from Mnemosyne's clutches as she tumbled to the ground. The magical object rolled toward Hades. It was almost as big as he was!

"Whoa!" he said, backing away. Before he could run, it bumped into him, knocking him over. In the blink of an eye, it shrank down to a size that would fit the head of a boy.

And for just a second Hades thought the helm flashed with gold and jewels! He blinked. When he looked again, he saw only a plain old spiked helmet. He must have been imagining things.

As Hades was getting to his feet, Zeus and Poseidon reached his side.

Poseidon snatched up the helm. He put it on his head and turned invisible. "We have the helm," his voice said gleefully.

CHAPTER SEVEN

The Furies

Hera jumped to her feet and wiped at her arms. "Eew! Dog slobber," she complained.

"Hera!" Demeter squealed joyfully.

"Demeter!" Hera squealed back. The two girls threw their arms around each other and hugged.

"Hera!" Still invisible, Poseidon wrapped his arms around both girls, making it a three-way hug. Since he only recalled half of everything, Zeus figured it made sense that he'd remember Hera, even if he'd forgotten Demeter.

But Poseidon also seemed to have forgotten how annoying he'd always considered Hera. That could be a good thing, though. Maybe there'd be fewer arguments between them.

Meanwhile, the Titans tried to sneak away. The dog was watching and quickly nabbed them again. Then it pinned them to the ground with its front paws. It grinned over at Hades, and made that happy gurgle sound again. "Sir. Brr. Us."

Though wary of the dog, the others gathered near it. After the boys explained to the girls about the oracle sending them on this quest for the helm, they made plans.

"I say we imprison these two Titans in Tartarus first thing," said Hera. Demeter nodded.

"Sounds good," said Hades. "After that we can look for the lord of the Underworld and return the helm to him."

"Or *her*," Hera put in.

"Come on, then," said Poseidon's disembodied voice. "Zeus knows the way."

"Of course he does," said Hera, rolling her eyes.

"You're welcome," Zeus huffed in reply as they all began walking. By now she'd hugged everyone but him. He was feeling left out. Not that he actually *wanted* a hug, of course.

"For what?" she asked, frowning over at him. "Saving me? Humph! I could've saved myself. Without the slobber."

"Where've you been, anyway?" Hades asked her.

"I got caught in an ocean current while looking for the trident," she explained. "Oceanus's doing. It swept me from sea to sea until I wound up in the River Styx. I've been trapped in the Underworld ever since."

As the group headed out of Asphodel Meadow, Zeus and Poseidon took the lead. Hera and Demeter were behind them, chatting away. Poseidon had given them the helm, and they were trying it on and giggling at being invisible.

Last of all came Hades and the dragon dog. The pooch carried Mnemosyne and Oceanus in its jaws like the two Titans were oversize dog toys.

"Go away. . . . Don't walk so close to me. . . . Stop breathing on me," Hades ordered now and then. But the dog just kept gazing at him with adoring puppy-dog eyes.

Every so often the Titans would start complaining, asking to be put down. But with a hard shake of his heads, the dog would shut them up.

A feeling of satisfaction settled over Zeus. "Four Olympians down, one to go," he said to Poseidon as they walked. "Only Hestia is still missing."

"You mean *five* Olympians down, right?" said Poseidon. "Including you."

Zeus's brow wrinkled in confusion. "Huh?" What was he talking about? Zeus was no Olympian! Thinking that Poseidon's memory was still half cuckoo from his River Lethe drink, Zeus decided to let the comment pass.

Just then Hera called to Poseidon, asking about his trident. For some reason, she eyed Zeus a little nervously.

Poseidon dropped back and proudly showed the trident off to the girls. "I'm god of the sea," he bragged to them.

Zeus couldn't help feeling a little jealous. Someday he'd have to give up his thunderbolt to that Goose guy it belonged to. But Poseidon would get to keep his trident forever.

As they all approached the dreaded pit of the Underworld—Tartarus—Hera accidentally dropped the helm.

"Careful," Zeus cautioned. "That helm's got powerful magic."

"Okay, Mr. Bossy Bolts," she told him. "You carry it. It's heavy." She tossed the helm to him and he caught it.

At the exact same time the dragon dog suddenly spit out the two Titans. *Patooey! Patooey!* It started barking wildly.

The Titans scrambled to their feet, ready to run for it. But Poseidon and Zeus drew their trident and thunderbolt, keeping them in check.

"What is that weird dog of yours barking at?" Poseidon asked Hades.

"It's not mine!" Hades said quickly. One of

the dog's heads stopped barking long enough to reach over and give Hades a lick, as if to say, *Of course I am.*

"Well, he sure has taken a licking—I mean, a liking—to you," teased Hera.

"Ha-ha," grumped Hades.

"Hey! What are those?" asked Demeter. She pointed upward. Three winged creatures were flying above them!

Mnemosyne squinted at them, then paled. "Oh, no! It's the Furies."

"Is that bad?" asked Hera.

"They're Creatures of Chaos!" Oceanus bellowed. "Of course it's bad."

As the Furies flew closer, Zeus saw they were women. One had a long pointy nose, another wore black pointy boots, and the third one had pointed ears. All three had wild hair and wore long black dresses. The belts and bracelets they had on were woven of live snakes!

The Furies circled overhead, gazing suspiciously down at the group on the ground. Finally each of them screeched out a question.

"Who goes there?"

"Why are you here?"

"What do you want?"

"We're Olympians!" Hades replied.

"We're taking prisoners to Tartarus," Hera added.

"We don't want any trouble," Zeus said in answer to the third question. He was hoping he could reason with them.

That had been impossible with the Androphagoi, the last Creatures of Chaos they'd tangled with. They'd had mouths in the middle of their chests and sharp, bone-crunching teeth. Brandishing clubs and spears, they'd attacked without asking any questions.

But it seemed that the Furies weren't interested in reason either. When they noticed the helm in Zeus's hands, they chorused furiously, "Thieves! You have stolen the helm. You must be punished!"

All at once the winged women dive-bombed them. Everyone started to run.

"Do something! Use your thunderbolt," Hera urged Zeus.

"Its magic doesn't work in the Underworld," Poseidon called back, without thinking.

Hearing this, the two Titans looked at each other. Then Zeus saw them look at the helm. It must be more powerful than anyone knew, since they wanted it so badly. Badly enough to stick around in hopes of surviving the Furies and stealing it back.

Luckily, the dragon dog's three heads were keeping the Furies at bay by snapping at them. For now at least.

"Leave us alone!" Zeus hollered to the Furies as he ran. "The Titans stole the Helm of Darkness. Not us."

Mnemosyne got a crafty look on her face. "They're lying! These five spawns of evil came here on a quest to steal the helm. Right, Oceanus?"

Oceanus hesitated, then nodded. He wasn't all bad, Zeus knew. But he was easily influenced by the other Titans, especially King Cronus. And apparently by Mnemosyne, too.

Mnemosyne jabbered on to the Furies, telling lies. "In fact, we saw them steal it. From the jeweled box on the throne that awaits the true lord of the Underworld."

"No! We're innocent," said Demeter.

Confounded, the Furies flew around and around the group.

"If someone doesn't confess, we'll drive you all into a river of lava," Pointy-Boots threatened.

"No! I say we dump them all in a sulfur swamp," said Pointy-Ears.

"I say we put a pox on them," said Pointy-Nose. She drew back and hurled what looked like a handful of beans at them.

They struck the dragon dog. Immediately it began scratching. She'd hit it with a pox of fleas!

"Idiot! You missed," Pointy-Boots complained.

"Did not."

"Did too. You should have hit the thieves, not their dog."

And with that the three Furies began fighting among themselves. They whipped their snakes around, clawing at one another.

"See?" Hades panted to Zeus as they continued to run. "This is why I liked it in Cronus's belly. No Creatures of Chaos. No Titans. No trouble. But then you had to come along and free us."

"It was a prison!" said Zeus.

"It was better than being chased by Furies," insisted Hades.

"True," Poseidon agreed. "In the king's belly we only had to dodge the occasional fish bone or incoming Olympian. I'm still glad we're out, though."

"Well, I'm not." Hades frowned at Zeus. "And Hera's right. You *are* bossy!"

And just like that, the boys started fighting too.

CHAPTER EIGHT

Tag! You're Dead.

"Stop it, you dweebs!" Hera yelled at the three boys.

But the Furies' anger seemed to have infected them. The boys began throwing punches. Poseidon swung his trident. Zeus drew his bolt. Hades snatched the helm from Zeus and slung it at the other two.

As they all struck out at the same time, the three objects they held connected. *Zap! Fizz! Zing!*

Suddenly the thunderbolt sparked with wild electricity. The spark spread to the trident and then the helm. All three began to glow with a magical golden light. Then the helm transformed before Hades' eyes, flashing with jewels. He dropped it like a hot potato.

Surprised, the boys jumped apart. Instantly the spark of magic faded.

"What just happened?" Hades wondered.

"Yeah, I thought you said your weapons' magic didn't work in the Underworld," said Demeter.

"It didn't. Until now," said Poseidon. "When they touched."

Before Hades could grab the helm from the ground, the dog dashed over and made off with it. No one else seemed to have noticed the flash of jewels, Hades realized. And the jewels were gone now. What was going on here?

"It may have been magic, but it was weak," said Zeus. "Not powerful enough to defeat those Furies."

"Well, that's really too bad," said Hera, pointing upward. "Because they've stopped fighting now. And it looks like they're coming in for the kill!"

Zeus, the Olympians, and the dog took off running again. They were right behind the Titans.

Sulfur smoke was all around them now. The pit of Tartarus lay dead ahead. The Furies were herding them into it! But at the last second the winged creatures backed off, circling overhead again. Zeus and the others stopped on the brink of the pit, huddling together.

"We have decided to give you a task as punishment," announced Pointy-Boots.

"Evildoers always fail at our tasks," said Pointy-Nose.

Pointy-Ears nodded. "So we'll figure out who's lying soon enough."

"I'll choose the task," said Pointy-Nose. "I'm very creative when it comes to punishments. Remember the time I put a pox on—"

"Ack! I'm the creative one," interrupted Pointy-Boots. "Remember the never-ending task of sorting asphodel seeds I gave those shades last month? Now *that* was creative!"

"It's nothing compared to what I did to those troublemaking shades last week," insisted Pointy-Ears. "Making them balance for hours on their heads and say tongue twisters while I tickled their feet with a feather? Classic."

Their captives listened in horror.

"I feel kind of woozy," said Demeter.

"Me too," said Poseidon.

Zeus stared into the pit of Tartarus. "I think

it's the stinky sulfur fumes coming from down there."

Oceanus nodded, and Mnemosyne fanned her nose.

"I like the stink," said Hades. "It helps me think. And here's what I'm thinking now: Since those Furies are trying to one-up one another with punishment ideas, I say we give them an idea of our own."

He winked at Zeus. Then he said extra loudly, "I hope the Furies don't choose a game as our task. Games terrify me. Especially a game like, um—"

"Tag?" suggested Zeus.

"Right," said Hades. Then he hissed at the others, "C'mon. Pretend you're scared of tag."

"Oh, no! Not a game of tag!" wailed Hera, catching on.

She elbowed Poseidon, prompting him to add, "Um, yeah, not tag!"

"Please, we beg of you," Demeter shouted. "Anything but that!"

As the Furies gathered to whisper together in midair, the Titans didn't speak. But the two of them were looking mighty nervous.

Then the Furies began to fly in circles again. Pointy-Boots peered down at all of them. "We have decided your punishment!" she proclaimed. "You must survive a game of tag. With Thanatos."

"Doesn't sound bad," Hera murmured.

"Yeah, I'm good at tag," Demeter whispered back.

Zeus nodded. "Me too." He'd outrun hundreds of thunderbolts back home on the Greek island of Crete. For some reason, until he'd gotten Bolt, thunderbolts had always been out to get him.

"This'll be a cinch," Poseidon added.

"You think so?" scoffed Mnemosyne.

Watching the three Furies still circling high overhead, she looked terrified.

She must know something that the rest of us don't, thought Zeus. It didn't take long to find out what that was.

Suddenly the Furies chanted: "Come forth, Thanatos, Bringer of Death!"

Zeus, the Titans, and his companions all looked at one another. That did not sound good.

"I have come!" boomed a voice in immediate reply. A man appeared from the gloom overhead and slowly sank to the ground.

No taller than a mortal man, he wore a billowing cape as gray as fog. Its hood hung low on his head, so you couldn't see his face. Except for his eerie smile.

Thanatos bowed to the Furies. "Ladies, I'm honored you have chosen me to execute this punishment. He grinned. And I *do* mean execute.

There's nothing I like better than a game of Tag! You're Dead." He rubbed his hands together and scanned his victims.

Zeus gulped. "You mean if you tag us, we fall down dead? Really and truly dead? Never-leave-the-Underworld-again dead?"

"You got it," said Thanatos. That creepy smile of his got even wider. He whipped his arms high and began whirling in a circle. This sent a gust of wind whooshing their way. It blew all seven of them—and the dog—into the pit of Tartarus.

And then they were falling. Not at normal speed but in slow motion, like they were in a dream. Or more like a nightmare. They went deeper and deeper and deeper.

When they landed at the bottom of the pit, the dragon dog dropped the helm. Before Hades could grab it, the dog snatched it up again and galloped off.

"Come back here, you crazy dragon dog!" he called. The smell of sulfur was thick around them. It seemed to have killed off the fleas. But though the dog had stopped scratching, it was too busy investigating everything to obey orders. And it still had the helm in its jaws.

Just then Thanatos dropped down into the pit too. When his feet touched the ground, he spoke to them in his eerie voice. "Game's on! Better start running."

And with that, the most terrifying game of tag ever played began. Thanatos was "it" and he chased them all, swooping and diving.

The Olympians and Titans slipped and slid in ooky globs of swampy stuff, trying to get away from him. Tartarus was even gloomier and stinkier than all they'd seen before in the Underworld. No flowers, trees, or plants grew here. Their only hiding places were behind sharp obsidian rocks that jutted from the ground like tombstones.

And the dog was no help to them. He kept bounding around the pit, acting like he thought this new game was all in fun.

The three boys and two girls spread out, each taking cover as best they could. So did the Titans.

"Thanatos is toying with us," Zeus told Hades as he ran past him. "I'm sure he's hoping we'll get tired sooner or later. Then he'll move in for the tag—er, kill."

A few minutes later Hades spotted Hera a dozen feet away. She was crouched behind a lava rock. Thanatos was sneaking up on her, looking like he meant business.

"Run, Hera!" Hades cried out.

Thanatos whipped around. Hera escaped. But now Thanatos set his sights on Hades instead.

Feeling powerless to help, Zeus watched Hades face off against the hooded Death guy. Slowly Hades was forced into a corner between two large hunks of rock.

"Back off," Hades told Thanatos. But the tremor in his voice betrayed his fear.

Grinning, the Bringer of Death crept closer. His long gray fingers reached out. They came closer. And closer. Until a gray fingertip was only an inch away from Hades' cheek.

"Tag," Thanatos whispered softly. "You're—"

CHAPTER NINE

Lord of the Underworld

But Thanatos never got to finish saying, *You're dead.*

Just as he was about to tag Hades, the dog made that gurgle again. "Sir. Brr. Us." He jerked his chin up, flinging the helm in a high arc through the air.

Hades stretched out his arm and grabbed the helm as it zoomed by. The moment he touched it, the helm transformed into a dazzling jeweled crown!

Seeing this, Thanatos stopped dead still. So did Hades. So did everyone else. They all stared at the crown in amazement.

So I wasn't imagining the flash of gold and jewels when I touched the helm before, thought Hades. Quickly he set the crown on top of his head. "Am I invisible?"

"Yes!" Zeus called to him.

As the Olympians and Titans gathered around, Thanatos bowed low to Hades. That is, to the empty spot where he'd just been standing. "All hail the lord of the Underworld!"

"Who, me?" Hades' voice asked in surprise. Thanatos nodded.

Hades removed the helm and examined it.

It remained golden and jeweled. He set it on a rock. It turned back into a plain helmet. He picked it up again. Crown.

"So that's why that dog likes you," said Hera. "You're the lord of the Underworld!"

"And that must be why the sulfur in this world makes you think better," added Zeus.

"And why you like stink," Poseidon added.

"I am your servant," Thanatos said humbly to Hades. "What would you bid me do?"

"How about you call off this game?" Hades suggested. He put the helm crown on again, going invisible.

The crown, the invisibility, and the knowledge that he was lord of the Underworld seemed to make him feel suddenly powerful. "And keep your fog fingers off my friends from now on," he added.

"Yeah," said Zeus. To show support he and

Poseidon came up to stand on either side of Hades. (At least they thought they were probably on either side of him.) Hera and Demeter joined them.

"Your wish is my command, O lord of the Underworld," said Thanatos.

Just then the Furies appeared overhead. They flew above the group in the pit like vultures circling their prey.

"Lord of the Underworld? No way! They have tricked you, Thanatos," said Pointy-Ears.

"You're wrong," Thanatos replied. "The invisible boy is the one we've awaited—the true lord of this world!"

Hades took the helm off, showing them the fabulous crown it became in his hands.

"It's just some sort of magic spell," said Pointy-Boots.

"Punishment must be served," added Pointy-Nose.

The Furies zoomed on the currents of sulfurous air, cackling and loudly flapping their wings.

"Duck! They're going to attack!" yelled Hera.

Hades thrust his arm up, holding the helm high. "Zeus, draw your bolt," he commanded. "Poseidon, hold up your trident."

"What about us?" Hera asked.

"Yeah," said Demeter. "What should we do?"

"Um . . . slap hands with us," Hades told her. "Now let's high-five!"

At his command five hands (three of them holding powerful, magical objects) touched as one. *Zap! Fizz! Zing! Slap! Slap!*

Instantly the bolt, trident, and helm all sizzled with a tremendous power the likes of which they'd never before seen.

"Flippin' fish sticks!" Poseidon yelled.

"Helmtastic!" cheered Hades.

"Thunderation!" exclaimed Zeus.

"Amazing!" Hera shouted.

"Awesome!" said Demeter.

The five of them broke apart, staring breathlessly at one another. Stunned by this display of power, Mnemosyne and Oceanus cringed in fear. Even the circling Furies now seemed impressed.

"What just happened?" asked Hades.

"Teamwork," Mnemosyne pronounced in an awed tone. "Your magic. It's bolstered through the power of teamwork."

"It appears that these Olympians are even stronger than King Cronus feared," Oceanus murmured to her.

"Strong enough that they overcame the Underworld's resistance to Earth magic," said Thanatos, sounding impressed. "Normally the sulfur here drains away the power of all magic that enters the Underworld from the Earth realm. Prevents shades from sneaking in magical weapons."

Pointing toward the Furies, Hades shouted a bold command to the Titans. "Tell them the truth. Tell them you were lying before."

Mnemosyne and Oceanus looked at each other. Then Oceanus shrugged and gazed up at the Furies. "All right. We admit it. *We* stole the helm."

The Furies gasped. In awe of Hades now, they fell all over themselves trying to please him.

"Oh, let me be the one to punish the Titans for stealing your crown, lord of the Underworld," begged Pointy-Boots. "If it is your wish, I can peck out the eyes of these thieves in less than three seconds."

"I can scratch them to ribbons in two seconds," Pointy-Ears put in quickly.

"That's nothing! In one second I can give them a pox that will make them itch as if bitten by a thousand fire ants!" claimed Pointy-Nose.

Yet another pox, thought Zeus. *Must be her specialty.*

"Uh, okay, good to know," Hades told them. "For now, though, maybe you could just stick these two Titans someplace secure in Tartarus. Someplace they will never escape from."

The Furies gleefully carried out his orders, herding Mnemosyne and Oceanus off. After they were gone, everything got quiet.

"Now what?" asked Hera.

"We go back to Earth," said Zeus.

"How?" asked Poseidon.

"Allow me to assist," said Thanatos.

Zeus looked over, surprised to see he was still there.

Thanatos clapped his pale hands together.

Whoosh! A chariot drawn by four black horses appeared alongside them. The group of five quickly boarded it.

"Upon your return to the Underworld one day in the future, we will hold a coronation ceremony and show you to your throne," Thanatos told Hades.

"Throne?" Hera echoed. "He gets a crown *and* a throne?"

"Well, he *is* lord of the Underworld," Thanatos told her. "And that's what the god of this world is supposed to get."

"I guess," Hera said, pouting.

Hades bid farewell to Thanatos, who was staying behind. Then he patted the dragon dog on each of its three heads in turn.

"Sir. Brr. Us," the dog gurgled happily.

"I think I'll name you Cerberus," Hades told the dog. "Since that's what you're always saying.

And since it looks like you're going to be mine after all. What do you think, boy?"

The dog licked Hades' face with all three of his tongues.

"I think he likes it," Demeter teased.

Hades smiled. "Be a good boy, Cerberus. Thanatos will take you out of the pit. And I'll come back soon."

Then Hades called to the horses. "Away!" he commanded. And just like that, the chariot lifted off.

"Hey, I just thought of a joke Charon would love," Hades announced as they began to rise. "Why did the chariot wheel come loose?" Then he supplied the answer before anyone could guess. "Because it needed to be *Titaned*."

Laughter filled the chariot as it took them higher. Soon they were out of the pit of Tartarus.

Only a thick layer of dirt and rock overhead separated them from the surface of the Earth above. But as they approached the rock full speed, the chariot didn't slow.

"Stop! We're going to crash!" Zeus yelled as they rose perilously close. Some of the others gasped or screamed.

Crack! A hole magically opened in the layer of dirt and rock above them. The chariot cut through it. They were out of the Underworld!

They touched down safely on the hill overlooking the River Styx. Right where the boys' journey had begun that very morning.

The minute they all stepped down from the chariot, two things happened. The horse-drawn chariot headed back to Tartarus. And Poseidon's memory returned.

"Right foot. Left foot! I remember everything again!" he said in a delighted voice. As his words died away, a cloud of glittery mist appeared before them.

"Pythia!" Zeus exclaimed.

Demeter gaped as a face framed by long black hair appeared within the mist.

"Oracle," Hera told her before she could ask questions. "I'll explain later."

CHAPTER TEN

Olympians, One and All

The oracle's face glowed within the mist. She blinked as she took off her fogged glasses to polish them. Then she put them back on.

"Congratulations, Demeter, Hades, Hera, Poseidon, and Zeus." The oracle smiled at each of them in turn as she spoke their names. "You have succeeded in your quest. The Helm of Darkness is now in the right hands."

"You mean on the right head," said Hades' voice.

Zeus looked around. Where was he? Then Hades reappeared behind him, holding the jeweled helm. He'd slipped it on for fun.

Pythia gave him a slight bow. "I hail you, lord of the Underworld. It is good and just that you have regained your rightful throne."

"Wish *I* had a throne," said Poseidon. He sounded a bit jealous. Zeus understood since he'd sometimes felt the same way about Poseidon's trident.

"At least you've got a trident," Hera shot back. She sounded a little jealous too. "I've got nothing. Neither does Demeter." She looked at the oracle. "Will I ever get a magical object like Zeus's bolt. Or Poseidon's trident? Or Hades' helm?"

Before Pythia could think them ungrateful for what they *did* have, and for the help she'd given them so far, Zeus chimed in, "We're grateful to you for guiding us in our quests. But before you give us a new one, we have a few things we'd like to ask."

"Very well. I will allow questions," said the oracle. "But you may ask only three."

"Why only three?" asked Poseidon.

"Because three is the most magical number of things," Pythia said matter-of-factly. As if that should've been obvious.

"Please don't make that the first question you answered," Hera begged the oracle.

Pythia smiled. "I won't."

Phew, thought Zeus. He kneeled and picked five blades of grass. Three were long and two were short. He stood again and held them in his fist out to the others. "Longs get to ask a question," he said.

Luckily, he picked one of the long blades. So did Hera and Poseidon.

"Will Demeter and I ever get our own magical objects?" Hera asked, going first.

"Yes. In time," promised the oracle.

"What will mine be?" Hera asked eagerly. The oracle did not reply.

"You only get one question!" Poseidon reminded her. Looked like those two were back to bickering now that Poseidon's memory had returned, thought Zeus.

Quickly Poseidon asked the second question. "What do you see in our future?"

"The future is what you make of it," Pythia replied. "But dark forces are gathering. You must be strong. As one. A team. If and when all of the Olympians are united again, you will have the power to defeat Cronus and his evil ways. If you fail, the entire world will be lost to chaos and destruction."

"But, hey—no pressure, right?" Poseidon joked lamely.

No one laughed. From the grim set of his jaw, even Poseidon seemed to realize that the idea of a world lost to chaos wasn't a funny one.

Pythia glanced at Zeus since it was his turn now. He opened his mouth. He'd planned to ask about his parents. He really had. But for some reason another question fell from his lips instead. "Am I an Olympian like the others, or am I a hero in training?"

At this, the mist around the oracle seemed to glow more brightly. "You are both," she said gently.

"Sorry, I should've told you that you were an Olympian," said Hera. "I kept it a secret for too long. I wanted to make sure you were on our side."

Zeus had little time to consider all this before Pythia spoke again. "And now begins a new quest," she told them all briskly. "Next you must find the Olympic Torch, which rightfully belongs to the Protector of the Hearth.

"Find the torch, and you will also find more of those you seek. Only, you must go carefully. For with each of your successes, King Cronus fears you more. And I fear for *you* when you next come upon him. It will be soon. Beware . . ."

With that, the oracle faded from view. They were all silent for a minute, watching the magical glittering mist until it disappeared.

Then Zeus raised his thunderbolt high. He pointed it westward, and everyone looked in that direction. The sun was setting there in the

distance, on the horizon. The sky was so orange and pink that it almost appeared to be on fire.

"Onward," he called out in a clear, brave voice. "To adventure."

Poseidon raised his trident. Hades raised his helm. Hera and Demeter raised their hands. They all touched, doing a high-five that excited their magic again.

Zap! Fizz! Zing! Slap! Slap!

"Onward!" they shouted as one. Then they turned to head toward the horizon.

Whoosh! Suddenly a giant fireball soared through the sky overhead. It screamed downward, heading right for them!

"Take cover!" yelled Zeus. Everyone spread out, running. He leaped behind a boulder just in the nick of time.

Ka-BOOM! The fireball exploded as it hit the earth.

As the smoke and dust cleared, Zeus peeked out. His eyes widened when he saw what had happened. There was now a crater in the exact spot where he'd been standing only seconds ago. The remains of the red-hot fireball still sizzled inside it.

Had the ball of fire been sent here on purpose to blow him to smithereens? By who? He didn't know. But one thing he did know. He was going to find out!

Hyperion and the Great Balls of Fire

For our heroic readers
—J. H. and S. W.

Greetings, Mortal Readers,

I am Pythia, the Oracle of Delphi, in Greece. I have the power to see the future. Hear my prophecy:

Ahead I see dancers lurking. Wait—make that *danger* lurking. (The future can be blurry, especially when my eyeglasses are foggy.)

Anyhoo, beware! Titan giants now rule all of Earth's domains—oceans, mountains, forests, and the depths of the Underwear. Oops—make that *Underworld*. Led by King Cronus, they are out to destroy us all!

Yet I foresee hope. A band of rightful rulers called Olympians will arise. Though their size and youth are no match for the Titans, they will be giant in heart, mind, and spirit. They await their leader—a very special yet clueless boy. One who is destined to become king of the gods and ruler of the heavens.

If he is brave enough.

And if he can get his friends to work together. And if they can learn to use their new amazing flowers—um, amazing *powers*—in time to save the world!

CHAPTER ONE

Boom! Boom! Boom!

K *a-BOOM! Sssst!*

A fireball as big as a watermelon struck the ground and exploded in flames. It had landed only a few feet from Zeus! He and four other ten-year-old Olympians had all been sleeping in a small forest at the edge of an abandoned village.

"Yeee-ikes!" yelled Zeus. Instantly wide awake, he leaped to his feet.

"My sandal's on fire!" shouted Hades, hopping around.

"I'm on it!" Poseidon called. He lifted his golden trident, which looked sort of like a pitchfork—only cooler.

Whoosh! Three streams of water suddenly spurted from the three pointy tips of the trident, hitting Hades' foot. It was just enough to put out the sandal fire.

Hades looked from Poseidon to the trident in surprise. "Did you gain a new magical power when I wasn't looking?"

Poseidon nodded. "My trident can magically draw water from any source nearby. A lake, a pond, even from deep underground. I figured it out last night when I was wishing for a drink of water."

"Handy trick," said Hera. She and Demeter—the two girl Olympians—had woken as well.

"Especially since those fireballs are back again," added Demeter.

All five Olympians had been dodging the mysterious fireballs since the day before. However, for some reason the attacks had stopped at sundown last night.

Now that it was dawn, the sun was here again. And so were the fireballs.

"I think the Titans are playing some evil game with us," said Poseidon.

Screee!

"Like Dodge the Fireball? Let's get out of here!" yelled Hera as another flaming ball came screaming in.

BOOM! Sssst!

The Olympians took off just in time. They hurdled over rocks and raced across parched ground. *If only there were a finish line somewhere,* thought Zeus. A place where they'd finally be safe from harm. Was that only wishful thinking?

The future is what you make of it, Pythia the Oracle had told them. *If and when all of the Olympians are united again, you will have the power to defeat Cronus and his evil ways.*

It was because of her that they'd begun yet another quest. This time they'd been sent to find the Olympic Torch. But as usual with the oracle's quests, she hadn't given them any details. Such as what the torch looked like. Or who had it. Or why it was important to find it.

Screee! BOOM! Sssst! Another fiery ball struck the dirt right behind Zeus. A huge plume of fire and smoke shot up from the ground.

"Thunderation!" he yelled. Flames licked at his heels as he put on a burst of speed.

"Someone's trying to blast us to smithereens!" shouted Hades.

"Yeah," Zeus said, panting. "And I think I might know who that someone is."

"Who?" Hera called out. She and Demeter were right behind them.

Poseidon came last. Pausing, he aimed the tips of his trident at the spot where the last fireball had fallen. A spurt of water put out the fire.

Screee! Boom! Sssst! Another fireball landed to the right of the Olympians.

They veered down a road that went left. "Look. A temple!" shouted Zeus. He pointed to a white marble building surrounded by columns. It stood at the bottom of a hill. "Let's take shelter there."

Soon the Olympians were all safely inside the temple. Hera shoved back a lock of long, golden hair that had fallen over her face. "Okay, Thunderboy," she said to Zeus. "So who's after us?"

The irritation in her voice was impossible to miss. At least she hadn't called him Thunder-*pants*. Another of her many nicknames for him.

Zeus shrugged. "It's only a guess. But I think it could be the work of one of the Titans I saw with Cronus. That day I made him barf."

Until recently the other four Olympians had all been imprisoned in the belly of the evil King Cronus. But after Zeus had sent a thunderbolt down the giant Titan king's throat, the king had barfed them all up.

Unfortunately, most of them had been recaptured by the Titans. They'd had to be rescued all over again, one by one. Zeus had seen to that.

But there was still another Olympian left to rescue. A girl named Hestia.

"The Titan I'm thinking of has a head that glows like the sun," said Zeus.

"Hyperion!" Demeter exclaimed, her green

eyes flashing. "That would make sense. He's the Titan god of light. The physical incarnation of the sun."

"The fizzy-calling-car what?" asked Poseidon.

Hera rolled her eyes. "Duh. It means he sort of *is* the sun. In bodily form."

They all ducked as they heard another fireball hit the ground somewhere outside.

"Does he hurl fireballs—er, sunballs?" Hades asked.

Zeus looked around for Hades but didn't see him. He must've put on his Helm of Darkness. It was a jeweled crown that made him invisible.

"Maybe," Zeus replied. "But no matter *who* is after us, we still have an Olympic Torch to find." He stood up and went to peek out one of the temple's windows.

"I'm betting that when we do find it, we'll also find Hestia," said Poseidon. "Because remember what the oracle told us: 'Find the torch, and you will also find more of those you seek.'"

"Right," said Hera. "Pythia also said the torch belongs to the Protector of the Hearth. Maybe that's *me*."

"Or me," Demeter said evenly. Both girls were a little annoyed that the boys all had magical objects. Zeus had a lightning bolt. Poseidon, a trident. And Hades, a helm. Yet the girls still had nothing.

Zeus patted the small thunderbolt tucked under his belt. It sparked at his touch. Although many had tried before him, only he had managed to pull it from the big cone-shaped stone in Pythia's temple. It was dagger-size now, but he could make it five feet long if he wanted.

"You know, I used to think my bolt belonged to someone named *Goose*," he told the others. At the silly name, Poseidon snickered and Hades smirked. The girls grinned.

"Only because that's what Pythia said the first time I met her," Zeus added quickly. "But it looks like she meant me all the time."

Demeter nodded. "*Goose. Zeus.* They'd be easy to confuse. Sounds like it was just another of her foggy-spectacle mistakes."

Yes, thought Zeus. And that meant the thunderbolt was really and truly his. It also meant he was the *leader* of the Olympians. Pythia had said so. He wasn't sure he *wanted* to be their leader. But since it was his destiny, he'd try to do his best.

Suddenly, loud shouts, heavy footsteps, and the clank of armor alerted the five Olympians to danger.

"Soldiers are coming!" hissed Hades' disembodied voice. "I can see them out front through the window."

Everyone looked at Zeus. "Should we fight them or run?" asked Poseidon.

Zeus hesitated. With their magical objects the boys could most likely ward off the Cronies. (That was what everyone called King Cronus's soldiers.) They might even be able to make the soldiers retreat.

"What? No answer, Mr. Smarty Thunderpants?" Hera asked.

Argh! There she went with those nicknames again, thought Zeus.

"Better if we escape before the Cronies figure out we're here," he decided. "Less risk of being captured or followed."

He could see daylight shining in through a hole at the bottom of the back temple wall. The hole was singed around the edges. Probably made by a fireball hitting the temple. And it looked just big enough for them to wiggle through.

"We can go out through that hole. Hurry!"

CHAPTER TWO

The Missing Torch

Zeus was last to escape out the fireball hole. And just in time too. As he wriggled through, he heard the Cronies. They were stomping up the front steps of the temple.

"Let's check in here!" he heard one of them shout.

It was Lion Tattoo! Zeus realized. He was the leader of the three half-giants who'd kidnapped Zeus in Crete. Zeus had escaped them more

366

than once. Good thing too, since they were always threatening to fry, grill, or toast him for a snack!

Once Zeus was outside, he raced to join his friends. Lucky for him none of the soldiers had come around to the back of the temple. Yet. But up ahead his fellow Olympians were nowhere in sight.

"This way!" a voice whispered. Hera sprang up from behind a large boulder, surprising him.

Zeus grinned at her. "Waiting for me?" he asked.

She rolled her eyes. "*Someone* had to, Bolt-brain. So you wouldn't get lost."

Boltbrain? That was a new one, thought Zeus.

Together they took off running. They had to hop over lots of big dents in the road where fire-balls had struck. The temple was soon lost to view as they rounded a hill.

Spotting Hades, Poseidon, and Demeter up ahead, Zeus and Hera caught up to them. From there they all wandered through one empty village after another. The farther they traveled, the more the sun beat down. It baked everything it touched.

After a while they came upon yet another small village. It looked as abandoned as all the rest.

Hera peeked in a door that someone had left open. "Hello? Anybody home?" she called out.

"They left. Wouldn't you? This place is fried," said Poseidon, fanning himself.

Demeter bent to stroke the leaves of a withered wildflower. "Poor little thing," she said. At her touch the purple flower perked up on its stem a little. When she let go, it wilted again.

Seeing this, Zeus's eyes widened. Was her touch somehow magic?

"Look! A water well!" Poseidon yelled. He

ran ahead to the well in the village center and looked inside it. Then his shoulders drooped. "It's empty."

Zeus hadn't realized how thirsty he was until now. Occasional sips of water from Poseidon's trident weren't enough. He went over to stare down into the well too.

"Can you fill it?" he asked.

"I'll try," said Poseidon. Holding tight to the handle of his trident, he lowered its three-pointed end over the side of the well. "Long!" he commanded. Instantly the trident began to lengthen.

When its sharp prongs reached the bottom of the well, Poseidon commanded it to drill. Spinning in superfast circles, the trident obeyed. It drilled down through the earth, going deeper and deeper. Minutes later water bubbled up, swiftly filling the well.

"Hooray!" Hera grabbed a terra-cotta jug from several that sat beside the well. She filled the jug with water and took a long drink. Then she passed it around to the others.

"Flippin' fish lips! That's good!" Poseidon declared when it was his turn to quench his thirst.

"Better than the water from the River Lethe?" Zeus asked. Poseidon had drunk half a glass of water from that Underworld river during their last quest. It had temporarily made him forget half of everything he knew.

"Huh? What River Lethe?" Poseidon joked now. "I don't remember it."

Zeus and the others laughed.

"Shh," Hades said suddenly. "I hear some-thing."

The five Olympians froze. Zeus's eyes scanned the far end of the village road. He expected to see Cronies. But instead a group of tired travelers appeared.

"Water!" one of them shouted. The whole bunch of them swarmed the well. They grabbed jugs and scooped up water, then drank thirstily.

"My village ran out of water a week ago," a man in a blue shirt explained.

A woman nodded. "There's a drought where I live in Olympia, too. Hyperion took over a temple there. He's been scorching every village and farm field for miles around."

Zeus's eyebrows shot up at the mention of Hyperion's name. So he'd been right to suspect the sun-headed Titan!

More travelers came, including a family. The young children ran to look at Poseidon's trident. He twirled it over their heads. They squealed with delight as a shower of cooling water drops rained down over them.

"Where did you get that thing?" their father asked. "Is it magic? Rumor has it that Hyperion is collecting magical objects. For King Cronus."

"Heard he's already captured a magical flame," another man added before Poseidon could reply. "Now his soldiers are searching every temple in Greece for a magical torch that can hold it."

So that's why the Cronies had stormed the temple he and the others had hidden in, thought Zeus. They'd been after the magical torch, not the Olympians, for once! He wondered if the flame's and the torch's magic somehow became stronger when they were together. A package deal.

"Maybe that's why Hyperion started throwing fireballs," Zeus murmured, thinking aloud. "Hoping to scare someone into fessing up about where the missing torch is."

"Any idea where it might be?" Hera asked the men.

Zeus knew what she must be thinking. That they should try to find it before Hyperion did.

Of course, Hera was convinced that she was the Protector of the Hearth, the Olympian that Pythia had spoken of in her prophecy. Which would mean the Olympic Torch would be Hera's magical object.

But Demeter was just as sure that the prophecy referred to *her*. Unfortunately, only one of them could be right.

"No one knows," said a woman in answer to Hera's question. "But once Hyperion has both flame and torch, he'll surely give them to Cronus. Who will turn their use to evil. Like he does everything else."

"Fireballs!" someone yelled suddenly. Everyone fled as three great balls of fire screamed down from the sky.

Zeus jumped over a low stone wall. He flattened himself against the trunk of a giant oak tree.

Just then the amulet that hung on a cord around his neck twitched against his skin. He pulled the smooth chip of stone from the throat of his tunic. The chip was as big as his fist. Like his thunderbolt it had come from the temple in Delphi where he'd first met Pythia the Oracle.

The other Olympians soon joined him in his hiding place. The five of them huddled together under the oak tree. They peered at the chip as the symbols that were now scattered across its surface arranged themselves into a map.

A small black arrow appeared on the map. It pointed toward a red dot labeled OLYMPIA.

"Flyin' fish sticks," said Poseidon. "That's where Hyperion is holed up! We have to go *there*?"

"Mm-hm," said Zeus. The chip guided them on all their quests. They followed wherever it led.

"But even if we *do* manage to steal the magical

flame from him, we'll need the torch, too, right?" said Hades. "Sounds like the flame must not work right without it."

"One of the villagers I gave water to told me about a temple south of here," Hera said, sounding excited. "Inside it there's a torch that refuses to light. I think it could be the Olympic Torch!"

"Maybe," said Zeus. "But Chip is pointing us to *Olympia*. In the north. Seems more likely the *Olympic* Torch would be there. If it's not, Chip will probably tell us where to find it. After we get the flame from Hyperion."

But as usual Hera disagreed with his plans. "By then it might be too late," she argued. "The Cronies are already hunting for the torch. They might beat us to it."

"How about if we split up?" Demeter suggested. "Hera and I can go south and look for the torch at that temple. You guys can go north and steal the flame."

"I think we should all stay together," said Zeus. "You don't have weapons. How would you defend—"

"Exactly!" Hera crowed. "Without weapons or magic of our own, Demeter and I can't help you against Hyperion. So you won't need us."

She had a point, thought Zeus. "All right, then," he said, seeing some wisdom in her plan. "Be careful, though."

"Humpf," said Hera, tossing her long golden hair. "We can take care of ourselves."

"Sure," quipped Poseidon. "Like on our last quest when you got captured and taken to the Underworld?"

Hera's face flushed red. But before she could think of a snappy comeback, another fireball came sizzling down from the sky.

Boom! Ssssst!

Crack! It hit the giant oak tree, splitting it. As the tree toppled, the Olympians yelled good-bye to one another.

Then the boys ran north toward Olympia, hoping to steal the flame. And the girls ran south, hoping to find the torch.

CHAPTER THREE

A Trio of Monsters

I t was mega-hot as the boys made their way north, following Chip's arrow. They tromped down dusty roads and across barren and rocky hills. Everyone they saw was heading in the opposite direction. Away from Olympia.

The boys had just caught sight of a mountain, when more fireballs blasted from the sky. But this time was different. The fireballs didn't explode when they hit the ground.

Instead they rolled up the road. Right toward the Olympians!

Poseidon's eyes bugged out. "Now Hyperion's *bowling* his fireballs?"

"Yeah. And we're the pins!" Hades exclaimed.

"Take cover!" yelled Zeus.

The boys dodged the balls and ran behind some rocks. So did several other travelers, including a young man with a beard.

Like most people they'd passed, he was carrying a big bundle on his back. Everyone was leaving the hot, dry places where they lived. They hoped to find cooler lands farther away, with water where they could farm and grow gardens again.

"Are you from Olympia?" Zeus asked the bearded man. "We heard Hyperion was there. We're looking for him."

Boom!

Just then the fireballs that had chased them exploded a ways down the road. An old woman sitting nearby let out a dry cackle of laughter. "You got a death wish or something?"

"Um, no," Poseidon said, looking alarmed, and a little bit chicken.

"Then if I were you, I'd turn around right now. Go back the way you came," the bearded man told them. "Fireballs are one thing. You can dodge those. But Hyperion's mere touch could fry you to a cinder! Nothing good can come from seeking him out."

Zeus gulped. "We have to see him, though," he said bravely. "We're on a quest."

Another fireball came crashing up the road. A gray-haired man dove in next to them, narrowly escaping being mowed down by it.

"Did you say 'quest'?" he asked, arching an eyebrow at Zeus. "Who sent you?"

"The Oracle at Delphi," Hades told him.

The old man gave a low laugh. "Pythia? I consulted her once. About buying some pigs. Instead she gave me some crazy advice about planting *figs*."

Zeus nodded. "She makes mistakes like that sometimes."

The old man grinned, as if remembering. "Worked out pretty well, though. I had years of excellent fig crops—till Hyperion came."

As the fireballs continued to rain down, the group stayed hidden. They shared what little food and drink they had. And they tried to sleep. At sunset the fireballs abruptly stopped. Just like they had the night before.

Once the moon rose, the boys crept out onto the road. Everyone else did too, all going their separate ways.

"Word to the wise," the gray-haired man

called to the Olympians. "Beware of the three creatures that guard the entrance to the temple Hyperion is using as his stronghold. Heard they're a dangerous lot."

"Thanks for the warning," Zeus called back.

As the three boys moved on, Chip's arrow glowed green, helping to light their way. It was pointing toward the mountain up ahead. Chip's map labeled it MOUNT CRONUS.

But when they reached the base of the mountain, there was a sign there that read: MOUNT KRONOS. The Titan king liked naming things after himself. But he was a horrible speller. Sometimes he even spelled his own name with a *K* instead of a *C* and substituted an *O* for a *U*.

"Stealing that flame won't be easy, you know," said Poseidon. As they began climbing, he was sounding more and more nervous. "I mean, Hyperion won't just *give* it to us."

"I know," Zeus said. "Don't worry. We'll figure something out."

"Think the dangerous creatures that guy told us about are more Creatures of Chaos?" Hades asked.

He was sounding jittery now too. And with good reason. King Cronus was always unleashing evil creatures on the world. It was like he was hoping to scare everyone into submission.

"Probably. But we can take them," Zeus said with more confidence than he felt. He figured it was a leader's job to encourage others.

"We've already done battle with a huge army of Androphagoi," he added. "What could be worse than monsters with sharp-toothed mouths smack dab in the middle of their chests?"

"Those punishment-obsessed Furies we met in the Underworld were pretty harsh too," said Poseidon.

"Right," said Zeus. "So compared to them, how bad could these three new monsters be?"

His companions paled. "Monsters?" echoed Poseidon.

"Oops. 'Creatures,' I meant," said Zeus. "Besides, don't forget we've got help. A trident, a helm, and this." He gave his thunderbolt a pat.

Hiking up the mountain was easier than it could have been. Because of the drought, there was no snow. Still, it took hours for the boys to reach the top. Once there they could see the city of Olympia in the valley down below.

"Look! The temple!" said Hades, pointing. Though it was still dark, Zeus was able to make out Doric columns. They surrounded the rectangular structure. Moonlight glinted off the roof's thin marble tiles.

As the boys set off for Olympia, they kept a lookout for the trio of dangerous monsters—uh, creatures. But all was quiet. By the time they reached the foothills, dawn was breaking.

They headed for the temple. They were almost to its steps when something swooped down from the sky to land before them. Its front half was a horse, but its back half was a winged rooster.

Hades made a sound that was part giggle and part gasp. "What is *that*?"

Was this one of the three creatures? wondered Zeus. If so, it didn't look all that scary.

"'Scuse me," said Zeus. "You're in our way." He started to go around the creature, but it moved to block him.

The creature stamped the ground with its two front horse hooves. It tossed its mane. "Neigh-a-doodle-do!" it said.

"Does that mean 'no'?" Poseidon asked it.

The creature scratched at the ground with its rooster claws, shook its rooster tail, and flapped

its yellow-feathered wings. "Cock-a-doodle-neigh!" it crowed.

The boys stared. Then they all started to laugh. They couldn't help it. This was the goofiest-looking creature they'd ever seen!

"Ha-ha-ha! What in the world are you?" Hades asked it. "A roosterdoodle?"

"Hee-hee. Or maybe a hooferdoodle? Or a wing-a-ling?" Poseidon asked.

The creature fixed them with an icy stare. Then it half-trotted and half-strutted toward them. "Whoodle doodle do you think you are?" it said in an annoyed voice. "If you think I look funny, have you tried looking in a mirror?"

"Whoa!" said Zeus. This caused the creature to come to an immediate halt. It acted as if there were reins around its horse head and Zeus had given them a yank.

"You can talk," Zeus said in amazement.

The odd-looking creature let out a sound that was half horse snort and half rooster squawk. "Of course I can. I'm a Hippalectryon, not a dodo bird."

"Hippa-what?" said Poseidon. He grinned at his companions. "Try saying *that* name three times fast!"

The boys began giggling again. The only way this monstrous creature was going to harm them was by making them laugh to death, thought Zeus. But their laughter was cut short when the Hippalectryon called for backup.

"Manticore! Onocentaur!" it whinny-crowed. Immediately two more creatures burst from around the sides of the temple. They stood on either side of the Hippalectryon, looking fierce.

The Onocentaur was similar to a centaur. Only instead of being half man and half horse, it was half man and half *donkey*. The Manticore

was scarier. It had the body of a lion, the tail of a scorpion, and the head of a man.

"State your business!" the Manticore ordered the boys. It had three rows of nasty-looking shark-like teeth inside its mouth. And it looked hungry.

Zeus considered those teeth. He also studied the sharp, pointy spines on the creature's tail. Were they poisonous? Just in case, he decided it might be best not to mess around.

"We're here to see Hyperion," he said in what he hoped was a commanding voice.

The creatures folded their wings, arms, and paws. They stared at the boys haughtily.

"And what makes you think that the High One, Lord of Light, Hyperion will want to see three little nothings like you!" brayed the Onocentaur.

"He's searching for a certain torch, isn't he?" Zeus said with a burst of inspiration.

The eyes of all three creatures went wide. In an instant they surrounded the Olympians. Suddenly they looked far more menacing. The boys didn't feel like laughing now.

"Doodle-do you have it?" the Hippalectryon demanded.

"I didn't say that," Zeus replied. He glanced at Poseidon and Hades. They nodded to show that they understood he was trying to trick their way into the temple. "But we might just have some information that—"

"Tell us what you know!" the Manticore interrupted. Its scorpion tail rattled menacingly. "Or else!"

"Oh, Manticore, give it a rest," said the Onocentaur. "Hyperion won't be happy if we slay them *before* he finds out the location of the torch."

"No, guess not," the Manticore said, sounding disappointed. "But maybe just one of them?"

"No! Now move it, boys," the Onocentaur instructed the Olympians.

"Unless you doodle-*do* want to become Manticore's breakfast," prodded the Hippalectryon.

And with that, the monstrous creatures ushered the three boys up the temple steps.

CHAPTER FOUR

The High One

Zeus, Hades, and Poseidon soon found themselves inside an enormous room within the temple. In the center of it was a huge marble statue of King Cronus seated astride a rearing horse.

"Wait here," the Onocentaur instructed them. Then he and his two companions disappeared into another part of the temple.

"Let's get out of here!" wailed Poseidon the minute the three boys were alone.

"No!" said Zeus. "We have to see Hyperion, remember? And somehow trick him into revealing the location of the flame so we can steal it."

"Zeus is right," Hades agreed.

To pass the time the boys began circling the statue that dominated the room, studying it. It nearly reached the ceiling of the huge temple. And it was so well sculpted that it almost appeared to be alive.

Poseidon pointed his trident at the statue's open mouth. "Cronus looks like he's shouting commands."

"To his army of Cronies, no doubt," said Zeus.

"Yeah, probably saying, 'Death to the Olympians!'" Hades shuddered.

Zeus eyed Poseidon's trident. "We'd better keep our magical objects hidden. So Hyperion won't try to take them."

"Good idea," said Poseidon. "Short!" he commanded the trident. Instantly it shrank down to only a foot and a half long. He tucked it under his belt, then arranged the folds of his tunic to cover it.

Worried that Bolt's occasional sparking might draw attention, Zeus removed it from its place at his side. After setting Bolt on the temple floor, he took off his belt, then retied it around his waist under his tunic.

Finally he tucked the bolt under his belt again so the tunic covered both belt and bolt. No way Hyperion would spot it now. At least Zeus hoped not.

"What should I do with my helm?" asked Hades. "It doesn't get any smaller."

Zeus rolled his eyes. "Do I have to think of everything? Put it on. Then it and you will *both* be hidden."

"Awesome idea!" said Hades. Two seconds later he and his helm went invisible.

Just in the nick of time too. Because a giant strode into the room right then. He was as tall as the statue of Cronus! And his entire head glowed like a pale sun.

"Hyperion!" Zeus whispered to his companions, recognizing the Titan instantly.

That night in the forest, when Zeus had thrown his thunderbolt down the king's throat, this Titan had saved Cronus from choking. And that's when the king had barfed up the five Olympians imprisoned in his belly.

Hyperion's eyebrows rose when he saw Zeus. "Good to see you again," he said. Then he smiled warmly. A little *too* warmly.

As the room heated up, Zeus began to sweat. Suddenly he wished he could take off his tunic. And jump into a lake. One that was full of ice.

In his mind Zeus quickly ran over the plan the boys had discussed earlier. It went like this:

Step one: Trick Hyperion.

Step two: Find the flame.

Step three: Escape with it.

Only now it struck him that the plan might've benefitted from a few more in-between steps. And some details about how to accomplish those things.

Hyperion switched his solar-heated gaze to Poseidon. "Well, if it isn't one of the barf boys," he taunted. "Looks like you managed to clean yourself up a little since the last time I saw you."

Luckily, Hyperion didn't seem to know that there were supposed to be *three* boys in the room. His goofy creature-guards must not have mentioned that fact.

Hyperion snapped his fingers. A golden throne magically appeared in front of the statue. He sat in it and got down to his evil business. "My guards say you have information about a certain . . . *object* . . . I've been searching for."

Zeus gulped. He racked his brain, trying to think of some way to trick Hyperion into telling them where he kept the flame. But before Zeus could get any great ideas, the Titan spoke again.

"But where are my manners? You boys look tired and hot. Lemonade, anyone?" Hyperion snapped his fingers again. This time a pitcher magically appeared.

Zeus and Poseidon eyed it thirstily and nodded.

Hyperion took a long gulp straight from the pitcher. "Ahhh," he said. "Delicious!"

The boys leaned forward. They licked their lips.

"Your turn," Hyperion said. He reached out as if to hand the pitcher to Zeus. Then he deliberately let it drop to the floor. *Thunk!*

"Oops, clumsy me," he said, laughing as the pitcher fell over on its side. Made of thick ceramic, it didn't break.

Before the lemonade could spill out and spread over the floor's mosaic tiles, Poseidon made a grab for his trident. "Long!" he shouted.

Zeus watched in horror as the golden trident lengthened. Seemingly unaware of what he'd revealed, Poseidon used his trident to suck up the lemonade. Then he drank thirstily as lemonade sprayed from the trident's middle prong like a fountain.

"It's good," he told Zeus. "Want some?"

Zeus groaned.

Hyperion slowly rose to his feet, his eyes gleaming. "That's Oceanus's trident!" he exclaimed. Oceanus was another Titan buddy of his and the king's. The boys had tangled with him on an earlier quest to a boiling sea.

Poseidon blinked, realizing his mistake. "No, it's mine," he countered, clutching the trident with both hands. "Oceanus stole it from me, but—"

"Well, it's *mine* now!" exclaimed Hyperion. Sparks and cinders flew from him as he reached toward Poseidon. At his fiery touch the golden trident glowed red-hot.

"Ow!" shouted Poseidon. He dropped the trident like a hot potato. It clanked to the floor as he blew on the palms of his hands to cool them.

Zeus lunged for the trident. But Hyperion moved faster. He picked up the trident, which looked the size of a fork in his big hands. The instant he grabbed it, it enlarged dramatically. It was now three times as long as Poseidon was tall!

"This will make a nice addition to the magical object collection I'm putting together for King Cronus," Hyperion said. His eyes burned into Zeus's. "Got anything else for me? Like that thunderbolt you had last time we met, perhaps?"

"Nope. I, um, lost it," Zeus lied. He could feel it under his tunic and just hoped Hyperion didn't have solar X-ray vision.

"Oh, too bad," said the Titan. He gave a low, evil laugh.

Zeus wasn't sure if Hyperion really believed him. Maybe he was just biding his time. Maybe he thought that if Zeus *did* have the thunderbolt, he'd get it off him later.

Regardless, Zeus was having second thoughts about using Bolt to fight the sun-headed Titan.

Hyperion's fiery touch hadn't melted the trident. But if his power clashed with the thunderbolt's electric charge, who knew what might happen?

"King Cronus will be quite pleased I've captured this trident for him," Hyperion said. With a snap of his fingers, a table magically appeared next to his throne. He set the trident on top of it. Then he plopped onto his throne again. "He was none too happy when Oceanus lost it."

"He didn't *lose* it," Poseidon argued. "I *took* it from him."

Zeus jumped when he felt a light tap on his shoulder. Hades whispered in his ear. "As soon as the trident cools down, I'll grab it off the table."

"Good plan," Zeus said.

"What's a good plan?" Hyperion asked. Apparently Zeus had spoken louder than he'd intended.

Zeus thought fast. "Um . . . your plan to collect magical objects for King Cronus. I'm sure he'll be grateful. Maybe he'll even make you his second in command."

Hyperion frowned. "I already am."

"Oh," said Zeus. Here was his chance to find out about the flame. "How amazing! You must be really good at getting things done. So, how many magical objects have you already collected?" he asked in a fake admiring tone.

"Besides the trident?" Hyperion replied proudly. "Just one so far."

"More like one half, actually." said Poseidon, sounding angry. "A flame without a torch, right?"

Hyperion leaned forward. His blazing eyes narrowed. "What would you know about that?"

"Nothing," Zeus said quickly. "Some villagers mentioned it. Said you need a certain torch to make it work?"

As he spoke, he noticed the trident move slightly. Hades must be over by the table trying to pick it up.

Hyperion smirked at Zeus. "And I suppose you know where that *certain torch* can be found?"

"Maybe," Zeus said. He had to keep Hyperion talking so he wouldn't notice the trident wiggling. "If I could get a look at the flame, I might be able to tell you if the torch I know about is the one you need."

"Uh-huh. Sure," Hyperion said sarcastically. "Pull the other leg." Looking skeptical, he started to stand.

Just then the trident rolled off the table. *Bam!* "Ow! Ow!" Hyperion yelled. The trident had hit his toe. He hopped around in pain, then bent and grabbed one end of the trident.

It jerked, trying to get away from him. "What the—," he said in surprise. He pulled it closer. It jerked away again. It was a trident tug-of-war!

Hyperion eyed Zeus and Poseidon suspiciously. "I don't know how you're making it move, but you're not getting it back."

Yanking hard on the trident, he managed to take it from the invisible Hades. He lifted it in his fist and then shook it in triumph at the two Olympians he could see.

"This trident is mine now. As are you. King Cronus will be very pleased at your capture." Glancing over his shoulder, Hyperion called out, "Guards! Come take them away!"

"Run!" shouted Zeus. He and Poseidon made a dash for the door. Too late. The three oddball creatures who'd brought them inside were blocking the exit.

"Call off the guards!" yelled a voice. It was Hades!

A look of confusion stole over Hyperion's face. "Who said that?" He glanced around the room. "Show yourself!"

CHAPTER FIVE

Lightning Strikes Twice

"Call off the guards," Hades repeated. He was still invisible.

"What magic is this?" Hyperion demanded, looking a little nervous.

He motioned for the guards to draw back. The Hippalectryon, Onocentaur, and Manticore moved away from the boys. But they continued to stand at the ready. Their wings, arms, and paws were flexed at their sides.

Hyperion's glowing eyes swept the room. "I did what you asked. Now show yourself, whoever you are."

"First you must return the trident to Poseidon," Hades ordered. Since the last quest, when he'd found out he was lord of the Underworld, he'd become quite bold. Especially when he was invisible.

"Oh, all right," muttered Hyperion. With an annoyed expression he tossed the trident back to Poseidon.

The minute Poseidon touched it, it shrank back to a size he could handle. But that didn't mean he *should* handle it right then. Because it was still hot.

"Yeowch!" yelled Poseidon. He tossed the trident from hand to hand as he waited for it to cool.

Meanwhile Hades removed the helm and became visible. He was standing right beside Hyperion's throne.

"The Helm of Darkness!" Hyperion exclaimed. His hands twitched as he stared at the glittering jeweled crown Hades held. "I thought it was hidden in the Underworld."

"It was," said Hades. "I found it there. Now it's mine." He stuck out his chest proudly. "Because I'm lord of the Underworld."

"Underworld, Schmunderworld," Hyperion scoffed. Without warning he made a lunge for the jeweled helm. "Give me that thing!"

"No! Toss it here!" Zeus called out to Hades.

Wasting no time, Hades pitched the crown toward him.

Zeus raised his arms to catch it. But as the helm sailed his way, the Manticore swung its scorpion tail high. The tail snagged the helm in midair!

"Thief! Give it back!" Hades commanded.

Poseidon thrust out his now cool trident. He

tried to use it to hook the helm off the Manti-core's tail. But the Manticore flipped the helm to the Onocentaur, and then wrapped its tail around the trident. It yanked. Hard.

The trident slipped from Poseidon's hands. Now the Manticore had it!

The Onocentaur brayed with laughter. The half man, half donkey set the helm on top of its head. "How do I look?" it asked its friends.

"Better than ever," the Manticore replied. "Because I can't see your ugly mug anymore."

The Hippalectryon flapped its wings and grinned. "Or the rest of youdle-doodle either."

"Stop goofing around, idiots! Hand those things to me this instant!" roared Hyperion.

The Onocentaur reappeared at once. Then it and the Manticore sheepishly handed over the helm and the trident. Both objects enlarged and glowed red in Hyperion's hands.

"Including these I now have *three* magical objects," he gloated.

"Well, two and a half, anyway," Zeus corrected.

"Whatever." Hyperion hooked his thumb toward the enormous statue behind him. "As I said before, King Cronus will be very glad to see them. And you three as well."

"Get them!" he ordered the guards.

"Do something!" Hades hissed at Zeus.

Left no other choice, Zeus whipped the thunderbolt dagger out from under his tunic and belt.

"Large!" he commanded. A sound like the cracking of a glacier rang through the room. Sparking with electricity, Bolt expanded to its full length of five feet.

Zeus stared Hyperion down. "Return the trident and helm!" Holding the thunderbolt, he drew back his arm. He was poised to hurl the bolt right at the fiery Titan.

"Looks like your lost thunderbolt just turned up," Hyperion said sarcastically.

Before Zeus could reply, Bolt was smacked from his hand. *Whap!*

"Yow!" the Onocentaur yelped as the bolt spiraled up into the air. The creature had kicked out with its donkey hind legs and knocked the thunderbolt away! But its legs had received quite a nasty electric shock in the process.

As luck would have it, Bolt went whirling up toward King Cronus's statue. *Thunk!* The thunderbolt stuck point-first in the marble king's open mouth. It lost its sizzle and glow the minute it lodged in the statue.

"Well, well, well," Hyperion said, chortling. "And they say lightning doesn't strike twice in the same place. King Cronus—the real one—

wasn't too happy when your thunderbolt went down his throat the first time. You escaped punishment then. But this time you won't be so lucky."

Turning his back to the boys and the guards, Hyperion stepped up to the statue. His eyes glowed as he reached for the bolt. "Now I'll have this magical object to add to my collection too! And once I have the torch, I'll deliver everything to King Cronus."

Hyperion gave the bolt a tug. Nothing happened. He tried again, tugging harder. But still the thunderbolt stayed stubbornly stuck.

"What's the matter, Your Brilliance?" taunted Zeus. "Not strong enough for the job?"

Hyperion pulled as hard as he could, muscles bulging. Still the bolt didn't budge. Because there was something "The High One" didn't know that Zeus did. Bolt couldn't be freed from stone—any kind of stone—without Zeus's help.

"Maybe you need to start doing push-ups," Poseidon chimed in.

"Better watch it or you'll soon be too weak to throw your fireballs," Hades teased.

Hyperion whirled toward them. His eyes went flat and hard. "Take them to the globe of destruction!" he ordered the guards.

The creature-guards surrounded the three Olympians again. "Don't even think about trying to make a run for it," the Manticore warned them. It gave its scorpion tail a rattle.

Zeus glared at Hyperion. "Let us go, you . . . you, glowworm! You can't keep us here. We're Olympians!"

"Olympians, Schmolympians," Hyperion sneered. "You're all a bit on the scrawny side for my taste, but Olympians are the king's favorite snack. As you well know. Take them away!" he ordered the guards.

Immediately the boys were rounded up and marched out of the room. "Down the stairs!" ordered the Manticore when they came to a set of steps. The boys stumbled down them as the three creature-guards followed behind.

The bottom of the steps opened up into another room underground. The boys' eyes widened when they saw what was inside: a huge flaming globe. It was about three times as tall as they were.

Zeus gulped. This had to be the globe of destruction Hyperion had mentioned.

With its back to the globe, the Onocentaur kicked at it three times with one of its hooves. *Kick! Kick! Kick!* A door appeared. The globe was hollow inside!

"In you go!" said the half man, half donkey.

Wings, arms, and paws herded the three boys inside. The fiery door slid shut behind them. The guards stomped away up the stairs again.

The boys were trapped. In a fiery prison!

CHAPTER SIX

Global Warming

Zeus slipped off a sandal. *Thwack! Thwack!* He hit at the place where the globe had opened. But nothing happened. Except that his sandal began to smoke from the heat. At least the floor under their feet wasn't fiery. Only the walls of the globe were.

"It's as hot as the Underworld in here," Poseidon complained.

"Seems just right to me," said Hades. "Nice

and toasty." Cold bothered him, but heat never did. "And anyway, we wouldn't be here if you hadn't lost your trident to Hyperion. *Twice.*"

"I was thirsty," Poseidon whined. "Besides, this is just as much your fault as mine. Why did you have to play the hero and take off your helm?"

Hades frowned. "Duh. To keep those guards from taking you and Zeus away."

"But if you'd stayed invisible, you could've followed when the guards brought us down here," Poseidon argued. "Then, when they left, you could've opened the door of this globe from the outside and—"

"We all made mistakes," Zeus interrupted. "I was dumb not to keep my thunderbolt hidden. Now none of us has a weapon!"

Pythia's prophecy said Zeus was the leader of the Olympians. But sometimes he doubted himself when he made mistakes like that. Did he truly have what it took to be a good leader? he wondered.

"What's done is done," he told his companions. "Arguing won't help. The thing now is to think of an escape plan."

"You're right," said Hades.

Poseidon nodded.

The three boys began pacing circles inside the flaming globe while trying to think up a plan.

"Maybe we could run from one side to the other superfast and *ram* through the globe door," Poseidon suggested.

Hades snorted. "Okay. You can be the first to try it. Zeus and I will scoop up your ashes afterward."

"You got a better idea?" Poseidon said with a scowl.

"Not yet," said Hades. "But *any* idea would be better than yours."

"I know!" said Zeus. Poseidon and Hades stopped arguing and turned to look at him. "The guards will return with food and drink eventually. After all, Hyperion needs to keep us alive."

"True," said Hades. "Till he can turn us over to the king."

"And so?" Poseidon asked.

Zeus grinned. "So when the guards open the globe, we'll trick them somehow and escape!" Abruptly his grin evaporated. "I haven't quite yet worked out the *somehow* part," he admitted.

Just then a tiny voice piped up. "Et-lip e-mip elp-hip."

"Chip?" Zeus had almost forgotten about the amulet. It didn't speak often, but when it did, it spoke Chip Latin. Which was like Pig Latin. Except that you moved the first letter of a word to the end of it and then added an *ip* sound, as in "chip."

Zeus lifted the amulet from around his neck. "Did you just say 'Let me help?'" he asked it.

"Es-yip," said Chip.

Poseidon and Hades came closer. The three Olympians gazed at the amulet with hope in their eyes.

"How can you help?" Zeus asked. "Do you have a plan? 'Cause we could really use one."

"E-bip ilent-sip," Chip said.

"Be silent?" Zeus glanced up at Hades and Poseidon. He put his finger to his lips. "Shh," Zeus whispered. "Chip needs quiet time to think of a plan."

"O-nip!" squeaked Chip. "Ilence-sip is-ip e-thip an-plip."

"'Silence is the plan,'" translated Hades. "What's that supposed to mean?"

Zeus thought for a minute. Finally he snapped his fingers. "I think Chip wants us to be quiet when the guards come back!" He stared at the amulet. "Right, Chip? Is that what you want us to do?"

"Ight-rip," said Chip.

"And then what?" asked Poseidon. "What's the rest of the plan?"

But now Chip clammed up and wouldn't say.

"Maybe Chip doesn't know the rest of the plan," said Zeus. He slipped the amulet back inside the neck of his tunic. "Maybe we'll just have to wing it when the time comes."

"We *winged* it before," Hades said glumly. "That's how we wound up here."

"Yeah, I know," said Zeus. "But—"

"Shh!" hissed Poseidon. "I hear something."

Sure enough they could hear hooves trotting down the stairs. The Onocentaur, Zeus guessed. Good. One guard would be much easier to deal with than all three.

"Lunchtime!" brayed the Onocentaur. Seconds

later the door to the globe slid partway open. The half man, half donkey tossed a leather water pouch inside. Poseidon caught it before it could hit the floor.

With one swift motion he pulled out the cork plug. He tipped the pouch toward him and drank, then passed it to the others.

The Onocentaur laughed. "Heat making you thirsty, huh?" The creature pulled a loaf of bread and a big chunk of cheese from a bag slung over its shoulder. It tossed those in too.

Hades caught the bread. Zeus caught the cheese. Holding on to the food, they stared at the Onocentaur but said nothing.

"Well? Aren't you going to say 'thank you'?" it demanded.

All three boys kept stubbornly silent. Suddenly Chip piped up. "Ank-thip ou-yip," it said in its squeaky little voice.

"Huh?" The Onocentaur looked from one boy to the other. "Who said that?"

The boys didn't reply. Their lips were zipped.

But Chip's weren't. "Ust-jip e-mip," it said.

The creature scowled at the boys. "I was watching all of you. How come no one's lips moved?"

The Onocentaur kicked at the fiery door with one of its hooves, opening it wider. It took a step inside the globe. "Is someone else in here, hiding behind you?" It tried to peer around the boys.

Staying silent, they scooted closer together, standing all in a row. The Onocentaur got even more suspicious. It rushed to the boys and pushed behind them to look for the source of the squeaky voice.

Catching Poseidon's and Hades' eyes, Zeus nodded toward the door. The creature was behind them and the door was open in front of them. This was their chance to escape!

Without a word the three boys leaped from the globe faster than even Zeus's thunderbolt could have flashed. The minute they were out, Zeus threw the hunk of cheese at the fiery door. It slammed shut, trapping the Onocentaur inside.

Bam! Bam! The creature brayed and kicked at the door, but to no avail.

"Yes! Trapped!" yelled Poseidon. "See how you like it in there, Your Donkeyship."

The heat from the door had melted the cheese. Before it could glop onto the floor, Hades reached toward it with the bread loaf. The cheese fell on top.

"Mmm, toasted cheese sandwich," he said, taking a bite. He broke off cheesy chunks and handed them to the others.

"Let's go!" Zeus called over his shoulder as he made for the stairs. Only it sounded more like, "Mesh gor," since his mouth was full of food.

Hades and Poseidon understood, though. They followed right on his heels.

Hyperion was nowhere in sight as the boys entered the upstairs room.

"Where do you think he is?" Hades whispered.

Poseidon pointed toward a window. "Sun's high. So he's probably off throwing fireballs at unlucky villagers. What I want to know is, where's my trident?"

While Poseidon and Hades began looking around for their stolen magical objects, Zeus ran to the gigantic statue. Quickly he shimmied up it.

Once he reached the top, he plucked his thunderbolt from the marble King Cronus's open mouth, as easy as pulling a knife from butter. Just in time too.

"You there! Halt!" The Manticore and the

Hippalectryon padded and trot-strutted into the room to confront them.

Zing! Zing! From his perch on the statue, Zeus whipped his five-foot-long thunderbolt back and forth in great swishes at them. They turned pale at the sight of the sizzling, sparking thunderbolt.

"He pulled it out!" cried the Manticore.

"Not even the great Hyperion was able to doodle-do that!" said the Hippalectryon. "We must inform him." With that, the two creatures turned tail and ran out of the room.

"Go get 'em, Bolt!" Zeus commanded. He released the thunderbolt. Happy to be free again, Bolt chased after the guards. Zeus scrambled down from the statue.

"Ow! Ouch! Yikes!" Zeus could hear the creatures yelling as his thunderbolt chased them, zapping them with glee.

CHAPTER SEVEN

Theia

I bet my trident's in here," said Poseidon. He thumped on a humongous wooden chest sitting in a corner of the room.

Well, it looked humongous to the Olympians, anyway. To Hyperion it probably looked the size of a jewelry box, thought Zeus. And maybe that's what it was. Or maybe it held the flame! Unfortunately, it was locked.

Getting an idea, Zeus whistled toward the

doorway. "Bolt! Come back, boy!" he called out. A few seconds later the thunderbolt zipped back to him.

"Can you cut through this lock?" Zeus asked the bolt.

Bolt reared back as if doubtful. Then, ignoring the lock, it sliced the top off the wooden chest instead.

After a stunned moment Hades said, "Good thinking, Bolt!"

Sparking with pride, the thunderbolt hovered nearby, waiting. Together the boys heaved the chest's sliced-off lid onto the floor.

When Hades and Zeus boosted Poseidon up to look inside, he gave a whoop. "Yes! I was right! The trident and helm are in there. Nothing else, though."

"I was kind of hoping the flame might be in there too," Zeus said. "But I guess that wouldn't make sense. It would burn right through wood."

Pounding footsteps alerted the boys that the two guards were coming back. And it sounded like the Onocentaur was with them! The boys could hear him braying in anger.

Using Bolt, Zeus thunder-pole-vaulted into the chest. He tossed out the trident and helm, and the other two boys caught them. Then he thunder-pole-vaulted back out.

The minute the boys ran outside, a fireball landed in their path. *Boom! Sssst!*

Zeus glanced up. He pointed. "It's Hyperion! He's on the roof of the temple!"

"Prepare to be toast! You'll never escape me!" yelled the sun-headed Titan. He wound up and pitched another fireball their way.

Boom! Sssst! This one exploded too close for comfort.

Despite their magic the bolt, trident, and

helm were no match for exploding fireballs. "Run!" Zeus yelled.

The boys ran. But the three creature-guards were also outside now. And they were blocking the way back up the mountain. The boys screeched to a halt.

They turned and ran the opposite direction. It wasn't the way they needed to go to meet up with Hera and Demeter again. But at least they'd be able to avoid the guards. And have less chance of being blown to smithereens!

Fireballs rained down on them as they fled. They darted from rock to rock and bush to bush to stay hidden. Finally, after several more hours, night fell and the fireballs stopped.

The boys wandered aimlessly through the forested foothills with only the moon to guide them. They grew tired and hungry and, eventually, lost.

"We failed," said Hades.

"Don't rub it in," said Poseidon.

"We'll try again. Don't worry. The magical flame will soon be ours," Zeus said. But this time it was hard to sound encouraging. He was losing hope himself.

"Hey! There's a light up ahead," Hades announced after a bit.

A flicker of hope rose in Zeus again. "Maybe it's the flame!"

They stumbled toward it. "No! It's a house!" said Poseidon as they drew near.

"Careful. This house is too big for mortals. Giants probably live here," said Zeus.

Still, the delicious smell of fresh-baked bread drew the hungry boys on, despite the danger. They stashed their magical objects behind a woodpile at the side of the house, then headed for the door.

Just as they reached it, the door flew open. A woman with a stiff, puffy hairstyle stood before them. Her brown eyes were heavily made up. And she was supertall. Titan tall.

Uh-oh, thought Zeus.

"Thought I heard the pitter-patter of little feet," she told them. "Come in. I've been expecting you!" Her unnaturally long, thick eyelashes gave a flutter.

Zeus blinked in surprise. "You have?" How had she known they were coming? Was this Titan an oracle, like Pythia? She didn't *look* like one. Pythia dressed in a plain hooded robe and had shiny black hair that hung to her knees.

"Of course," the woman said. "My husband promised to send me some servants." She pursed her painted red lips. "Only I didn't expect you to be so young. Or so small. But I suppose you'll have to do."

The woman's glittering golden gown rustled softly as she moved aside for the boys to enter. She adjusted her feather boa.

Poseidon crossed his arms, frowning. "We're not ser—"

"We're stronger than we look," interrupted Zeus.

He glanced meaningfully at Poseidon and Hades. He hoped they'd realize he wanted them to play along. It wasn't safe to reveal their true identities. Not yet, anyway. Not before they got some food and found out who this Titan lady was. Maybe never!

"Good," said the woman. She led the boys to her kitchen, where a small fire blazed in the hearth.

"My name's Theia," she said. "And your names are . . . ?"

"Goose," said Zeus.

Poseidon and Hades giggled.

Zeus turned red. In his haste to hide his true identity, the nickname had been the first thing to pop into his head. He wished he could take it back. But now it was too late.

Theia arched an eyebrow at him. "Your name's 'Goose'?" she said, sounding amused. "Your mother must've been feeling hungry when she named you that." She threw back her head and laughed.

"Yes, ma'am. I suppose she was," Zeus said. He pointed to Poseidon and Hades, who were both still smirking at him. It was time for a little payback, he decided. "And these are my friends, Fishbreath and Stinkboy," he announced.

The two boys scowled at him. Now it was Zeus's turn to grin.

Theia laughed harder still. "That's some sense of humor your parents have."

"Yeah," Hades said drily. "They were probably a couple of crack-ups."

"Probably? Oh, I'm sorry," Theia said gently. "Are you orphans, then?"

Immediately Poseidon pressed his hands over his heart, playing on her sympathy. "Yes. We are," he said with downcast eyes.

Good one, thought Zeus. Though in truth he didn't know anything about the other Olympians' parents. It was something they'd never discussed.

Theia clucked. "You poor things," she said. "It was nice of my husband to take you in and give you jobs, then." She gave her head a slight shake. "He does have a good side. It's King Cronus who's a bad influence on him."

The three Olympians darted nervous looks at one another. Zeus wanted to ask who Theia's husband was. But if he did, she'd know the boys were imposters—that her husband hadn't really sent them.

He gulped as a new thought came to him. What if the *real* servants arrived while the boys were still there? He hoped they wouldn't come until morning. By then maybe the boys would be fed and rested. And long gone.

He couldn't help glancing at the gigantic loaves of bread cooling on top of a table. *Mmm.* They smelled so good. He must've drooled a little, because Theia smiled at him.

"Hungry?" she asked.

All three boys nodded.

"Then help me get dinner ready," she said, putting them to work.

Poseidon started peeling potatoes the size of pumpkins for stew. And Hades struggled to wield a knife as long as a sword to chop carrots as thick as his arms.

Theia sent Zeus out to chop wood. The ax was way too big and heavy for him to handle. After checking to see that no one was around, he whistled softly for Bolt. "Come, boy. I need your help!"

On command Bolt zipped from behind the woodpile, all aglow.

"Okay. Let's get to work," said Zeus. He swung the thunderbolt at a thick chunk of firewood.

Crack! The wood split right down the middle.

"Good job!" Zeus said softly. At the praise, Bolt glowed even more brightly. Before long they'd chopped a nice stack of wood. It was a bit charred around the edges, though. He hoped Theia wouldn't notice.

As the thunderbolt hid again, Zeus took a load of wood into the cottage. There he added it to the fire.

Theia had hung a big pot full of water and meat over the hearth. Now she added the potatoes and carrots that the other two boys had chopped.

Hades and Poseidon had begun to set the table. Poseidon lined up silverware. Hades carried bowls as big as sinks to the table.

"Should we set a place for your husband, too?" Hades asked.

Theia laughed lightly. "No need . . . uh . . . *Stinkboy.* He won't be home tonight. Sent word he'd lost something and had to work late tonight to find it again. Just set places for yourselves and for me. Oh! And a place for Hestia, too."

CHAPTER EIGHT

Something Fishy

H estia?" echoed Zeus.

Poseidon uttered a strangled cry.

Crash! Hades dropped the bowl he was holding. It shattered against the tiled floor. "Oops! Sorry!" he said.

"Not to worry," said Theia. She kept on stirring the stew with a big wooden spoon. "Accidents happen. Just finish setting the table. I'll sweep up the pieces later."

"Um, is Hestia your daughter?" Zeus asked. He tried to sound casual. After all, there could be other girls named Hestia besides the Olympian girl they sought.

Theia laughed. "No. My children are all grown up. Hestia is my husband's—that is, *Hyperion's*—niece."

Poseidon and Zeus looked at each other with wide eyes. Hades dropped another bowl. *Crash!*

Theia looked over at him. "Maybe I'd better assign you a different task. Before all of my bowls are broken?"

"Sorry," Hades said again. "Guess I'm just clumsy tonight." He shot Zeus a glance and began picking up the broken pieces.

"So where is Hestia?" asked Poseidon.

Theia pointed with her wooden spoon to a room across the hall. "She's taking a nap. Such a nice girl, but very quiet. Hasn't said a word since she came here a few weeks ago. It's almost like there's a spell on her tongue."

Zeus peered toward the door she'd pointed to. King Cronus had ordered Hyperion to capture Hestia, put a spell on her, and hide her here. He was sure of it!

Theia honestly didn't seem to know that Hestia wasn't Hyperion's niece, however. His spell must have been keeping Hestia from telling the truth of who she was.

Just then the door across the way opened. A girl stepped out of the room. Her light brown hair was tangled from sleep.

Her brown eyes lit on Zeus first. He smiled, but the look she returned was vacant. *Lights on. Nobody home,* he thought.

But that changed the moment Poseidon and

Hades called out to her. "Hestia!" they exclaimed in joyful voices.

Her head turned toward them. All at once her eyes widened and became bright. Whatever spell had been holding her speechless fell away at the sight of the two boys.

"Poseidon? Hades? I thought I'd never see you again!" she cried out. She flew to the boys and hugged them. "But where are Hera and Demeter?" she asked.

"They stayed behind," said Poseidon, casting a wary eye in Theia's direction. She was gazing at them with suspicion now.

"Well, who's that?" Hestia asked, staring at Zeus.

Theia was staring at him now too. "You're Zeus, aren't you!" she exclaimed suddenly. "And you're all Olympians! You tricked me."

Braced for the worst, the four Olympians began backing away.

Theia pointed her wooden spoon at them. "Stop right there."

"Or what?" challenged Zeus. He'd hoped she would have a good heart, but he should have known better.

"Or you'll miss dinner," she said.

The Olympians looked at one another in surprise.

Turned out Theia *did* have a good heart. And she wasn't as completely trusting of Hyperion as they'd feared.

Over bowls of the delicious stew and thick slices of warm bread, the boys took turns explaining about their quest. They told Theia and Hestia how Hyperion had been wreaking havoc with fireballs and drought. They even brought their magical objects inside the house to show them off.

"Hyperion has stolen the flame that lights the Olympic Torch. The torch that the oracle Pythia sent us to find. Did he tell you that?" Hades asked Theia.

"No." Theia's lips tightened. "I thought I smelled something fishy."

Poseidon stopped eating, looking alarmed. "Is it me?" He sniffed himself. "It's probably because I'm god of the sea. Sorry, I—"

Theia interrupted him. "No, that was just a figure of speech," she said kindly. "I meant that I already suspected Hyperion was up to something." She glanced at Poseidon again. "Of course, I'd be lying if I said you smell as sweet as a rose, but— Well, never mind."

She ladled more stew into Zeus's huge bowl. He was so hungry, he'd finished off the first bowl in record time. "I met your mother once, you know," she told him.

Zeus's jaw dropped. "You did?"

Theia glanced around the table, then nodded. "She was a wonderful woman. And absolutely determined to keep you safe from harm."

"Is that why she left me in that cave on Crete?" Zeus asked excitedly. He'd long wondered about his parents, hoping to find them someday. "Is—is she still alive?"

Theia nodded again. "She's alive. And probably with Cronus, but I—"

Zeus sucked in his breath, imagining his mother locked up in a castle tower. Or in the depths of a gloomy dungeon. He jumped up.

"Then I'll rescue her!" he said fiercely. "Where is she?"

Stomp! Stomp! Stomp!

Before he could ask any more questions, they heard the stamping of heavy feet outside.

Theia ran to peer out a window at the front of the house. "Half-giants. Cronus's soldiers," she told the others. "Quick! I'll delay them while you all duck out Hestia's bedroom window in the back."

"Why should we trust you?" asked Zeus. "You're a *Titan*. Hyperion's *wife*."

"Your mother was kind to me," Theia told him. After grabbing an unlit oil lamp, she ran to kneel before the hearth. "I owe her a big favor. And now I'm going to repay it."

With those words she poked a long, thin stick into the hearth fire. When the tip of the stick burst into flame, she used it to light the lamp. But oddly, the moment the flames in the hearth had leaped to the stick, the fire in the hearth

454

had snuffed out. Only smoke remained to curl up the chimney.

Theia tried to hand the lamp to Zeus as everyone hurried into the bedroom. Clouds had moved in to hide the moon. It was pitch-black outside, Zeus realized. They would need light. But the flame in the lamp was dim now. And he was reluctant to take any gift from a Titan. Even a nice one.

"Take it," said Theia. "I'm almost certain it's the magic flame you seek."

At that, all four Olympians stopped in their tracks. Their eyes went to the lamp and they stared in amazement.

"The magic flame that lights the Olympic Torch!" Zeus exclaimed, catching on at last.

"It was here all along," said Poseidon.

"Hyperion hid it right in plain sight. In your hearth!" Hades added in a stunned voice.

Boom! Boom! Just then the soldiers pounded on the door.

"Yes. I'd seen him hide something there days ago, but didn't put two and two together until you mentioned the flame he'd stolen. Now take it and go," insisted Theia.

"Do as she says," Hestia urged. "She has been kind to me. I don't think she means us harm."

Oomph! Oomph! Hades and Poseidon leaped out the back window. As Hestia followed the boys out, Zeus took the lamp from Theia.

"I won't be able to help you after this," she warned him solemnly. "And I'll tell Hyperion you *stole* the flame."

"I understand." Clutching the lamp, Zeus ran for the window. "About my mother," he called back over his shoulder. "Where—"

But Theia had already gone to answer the

door. Frustrated at missing his chance to learn more, Zeus climbed outside. Then, with the lamp to light his way, he ran to catch up with the others.

CHAPTER NINE

The Journey Back

When Zeus caught up to his friends, he handed the lamp to Hades. Then he pulled up on the leather cord around his neck.

"I can't believe it! We got the flame!" Hades crowed.

"We are awesome!" said Poseidon. "Now let's just hope Hera and Demeter somehow managed to find the torch it's supposed to light."

Hestia smiled. "Ooh! I can hardly wait to see them again!"

The boys looked at Zeus, waiting for Chip's directions. Hestia stared at it curiously until Hades explained how it worked.

"That way," Zeus told the others after consulting the amulet. "Looks like we'll have to pass Hyperion's temple on the way."

"Not so awesome," said Poseidon.

But with no other choice the Olympians followed Chip's arrow. They stayed close together as they headed toward Hyperion's temple once again. The lamp's flame remained dim, but it helped light their way through the dark night.

Hestia had already heard much about their adventures at dinner. But as they traveled on, the boys filled her in on everything she'd missed while she'd been held captive.

"But why does the flame need to be contained

in a special torch?" she said after a while. "Why can't we just keep it in this lamp?"

"Well, the flame and the torch are both probably magic," mused Hades.

"I guess their magic gets super-charged when they're joined together," said Poseidon.

"But what does their combined magic do?" Hestia asked.

Poseidon shrugged. "Pythia didn't tell us."

"But it's bound to be something good," Zeus said. "Or she wouldn't have asked us to find it."

"It'll be something to help the villagers, I bet," said Hades. "Hyperion's fireballs have dried out the land. The drought has destroyed their crops. People are abandoning their homes."

"Then we must defeat him," Hestia said in a determined voice. "We must join the flame and torch together. And then we'll just see what happens!"

A few hours later the Olympians reached the valley. Hyperion's temple was dark and quiet. Giving it a wide berth, the four travelers crept on by. Then they continued up and over the mountain, to meet up with Hera and Demeter.

"That was surprisingly easy," Hades remarked.

Poseidon nodded. "Hera said Hyperion's sort of like the sun, right? So I think he must have to sleep at night. That's probably why the fireballs always come to a halt at sunset."

Zeus stopped to check Chip's arrow again. He handed the lamp off to the nearest person, who happened to be Hestia.

The minute she took it, Zeus noticed something interesting. The flame inside the lamp flared higher and glowed more brightly than ever before.

"Wow! That's better," said Poseidon.

"Yeah," agreed Hades. "Now we can actually see the path!"

As the Olympians moved on, Zeus thought about his mother. She was alive! Theia had said so. He could recall Theia's words exactly: *She was a wonderful woman. And absolutely determined to keep you safe from harm.*

But where was she now? Was she in danger? Had Cronus kept her prisoner all these years? Maybe because she'd refused to tell him where she'd hidden Zeus? That was so unjust! Zeus clenched his fists.

If he had to come face-to-face with King Cronus again to rescue his mother, then that's what he would do! As soon as he got the chance.

Around midnight the four Olympians neared the village where they'd last seen Hera and Demeter. They bedded down under some trees by the road near the village entrance.

At dawn they woke to the sound of familiar voices. *Hera and Demeter!* The two girls were walking toward them along the main road. Zeus and the others scrambled to their feet and went to meet them.

"Hestia!" Hera and Demeter squealed when they caught sight of her with the boys.

Hestia quickly handed off the lamp to Hades. Only Zeus seemed to notice that the flame instantly went dim again. The three girls jumped up and down and hugged one another.

"We were just coming to look for you," Hera told the boys after the girls had calmed down a little. "We didn't expect to find you so fast!"

"Look what we have," said Demeter. She reached into a bag she was carrying. She pulled out a long metal cone decorated with beautiful carvings. It's top was shaped like a shallow bowl.

"It's the torch!" Hera exclaimed.

Hades showed them the lamp. "And we've got the flame!"

Zeus's brow wrinkled. "But how do we know it's the right torch?"

"Of course it is," said Hera. "A priestess gave it to us."

"She said it came from a temple in Olympia," said Demeter. "One that Hyperion took over in King Cronus's name—"

"And guess what?" Hera broke in. "Before the Titans took over the temple, it was named the Temple of *Hera*." Her blue eyes gleamed. "Which must mean that the Olympic Torch is *my* magical object."

Demeter looked unsure. "Maybe." She glanced back at the others. "Anyway, Hyperion tried to force the priestess to hand over the Olympic Torch."

Hera picked up the story again. "But afraid of

what he'd do with it, the priestess tricked him. She separated the flame and torch, knowing that they only had true magical powers when united. She put the flame atop a regular torch and gave that to him instead."

"Then she fled the temple with this unlit magical torch we found," Demeter said. "When we told her about Pythia and our quest, she gave it to us. But she cautioned us that only the Protector of the Hearth can reunite the torch and flame again."

"What are we waiting for?" asked Hades. He held up the lamp. "Somebody try it and see what happens."

"I'll light it," Hera said eagerly. Reluctantly Demeter handed her the big, unlit torch. Taking great care, Hera held the torch over the lamp's flame.

Everyone leaned in, hardly daring to breathe.

Would the torch catch fire? Moments passed. The torch remained dark. The flame still burned dimly in the lamp.

Hera stared at the torch. Her shoulders slumped with disappointment. "What's wrong with this thing?"

"Let me try," Demeter said, reaching for the torch and lamp. But she had no more luck than Hera.

"Maybe the priestess made a mistake," said Hera. "Maybe this isn't the right torch after all."

"May I try?" asked Hestia. Her voice was gentle so as not to rub it in that her friends had failed. Yet there was a spark of excitement in it.

Demeter shrugged. "Sure. Go ahead." She passed the torch and lamp to Hestia.

The moment Hestia held the lamp close to the torch, the flame leaped to it. Everyone gasped as the torch immediately sparked high. Dazzling red, yellow, and blue lights wove together in a fiery dance. The six Olympians stared at the blazing torch in awe.

"Congratulations!" said an approving voice.

They'd all been so amazed by the torch that they hadn't noticed the vent that had opened in the ground behind them. In a glittering cloud of steam, the oracle Pythia's bespectacled face now rose before them.

CHAPTER TEN

Seeds of a New Quest

Hestia stared, wide-eyed, at the vision of Pythia. Clasping the torch to her chest, she took a step back.

"Oracle," Demeter whispered to her quickly.

"Oh," Hestia whispered back. "She's who you've all been talking about!"

"Well done, Olympians!" the oracle said. "You have united flame and torch and reclaimed the Olympic Torch at last. And now it is in

the hands of the Protector of the Hearth." She smiled at Hestia.

It was just as Zeus had suspected the moment he'd first handed the lamp to Hestia. That's why the torch had flamed higher and brighter for her than for anyone else. *She* was the Protector of the Hearth.

"The torch has great magic," Pythia told the Olympians. "And its flame can never die out. Already, in villages and towns across Earth, the torch's healing magic is causing people to return to their homes, their hearts filled with new hope for a better life."

She paused, peering out at them through her foggy spectacles. "Along with your other magical objects, this torch will serve you well and help you to help others in the difficult times to come. Especially as you continue to search for the remaining Olympians."

Zeus looked at her in surprise. "Remaining Olympians? But I thought there were only six of us. Me, Poseidon, Hades, Hera, Demeter, and Hestia. We're all here. Are you saying there are more?"

Pythia's eyes filled with a faraway look. Like she was remembering a truth that only she knew. "Yes. Cronus didn't swallow all of the Olympians," she replied mysteriously. "And so, you see, the quest must continue. For there are many more of you."

"How many?" asked Poseidon.

"But I was planning to search for—," Zeus started to say.

"Your mother is not in immediate danger," Pythia interrupted, answering Zeus. It wasn't the first time she'd seemed to read his mind. "You must gather the other Olympians before you seek her out."

She glanced at Poseidon. "As for their number, it is unclear to me at present."

Before Zeus could protest, or even ask his mother's name, Pythia threw her arms wide.

"Hyperion's actions have devastated the land," she said in a dramatic voice. "On your next quest you must repair it as best you can. You must find the Magic Seeds that will give this land new life."

"Where? How?" asked Hades.

"Use the magic you've already been given," she replied.

"Even if we repair the land, won't Hyperion just wreck it again with his fireballs?" asked Hera.

Pythia shook her head. "King Cronus wasn't happy to learn of your escape. Or that you'd reclaimed the flame. He blames Hyperion for losing the magic flame to you and has banished him." Her image in the steam wavered and began to fade.

"Wait! Don't go yet," Zeus called out. "Even if I must wait to see her, can you at least tell me my mother's name?"

"Mia," said Pythia, her image growing stronger again. "Or, hmm. Maybe it's Dia. Or Rhea. Or Leah. It's hazy. . . ." Then abruptly she disappeared.

"Hey, watch it, Hestia!" Poseidon complained suddenly.

"Oops. Sorry," she said. She'd put the bottom tip of her torch in the center of her palm and had set the torch spinning. While trying to balance it there, she'd accidentally bumped into him.

Zeus glimpsed Hera and Demeter watching her. Demeter's arms were crossed in front of her chest. And there was a pinched expression on Hera's face. Were they feeling jealous of Hestia? Like the boys, she had a magical object now. But the other two girls still hadn't earned theirs.

By now people who had long been away from home were gathering in the village center. "Something's changed," Zeus heard a woman say cheerfully. "I feel hopeful again. And glad to be home."

Another man nodded. "Me too. Though a great big thunderstorm would be nice. To make things grow again."

A *thunder*storm? thought Zeus. Pythia had said they should help repair the devastated land. *Use the magic you've already been given,* she'd said.

Zeus pulled Bolt from his belt. "Large!" he commanded. In an instant the thunderbolt expanded to its full length. Zeus drew back his arm. Then he sent Bolt flying toward the only cloud in the sky.

When the thunderbolt hit the cloud there was a loud crash. The sky darkened. Other clouds formed. Sparking and sizzling, Bolt zoomed from one cloud to another. Soon booms of thunder and flashes of lightning filled the entire sky.

All at once the heavy clouds dumped their precious load.

The Olympians and villagers dashed for cover as rain fell everywhere. It drummed the roofs of the houses. It fed the parched fields. And it collected in all the pots and urns around the well. And yet it didn't even dim the flaming torch that Hestia still held.

Having done its work, Bolt zoomed back to Zeus. The clouds stopped raining.

Awestruck and grateful, the villagers cheered

the Olympians. "Hooray! Thank you!" they cried out.

Would his mother have been proud of him if she could have seen what he had accomplished? Zeus wondered. He knew that more would be needed to heal the land. But this was a start. Next they needed to find those seeds Pythia had spoken of.

"Where to now, Thunderboy?" Hera asked. She was smiling at him for once, seeming pleased at what he'd done. They were all feeling pretty good now, having successfully completed their quest and having brought rain to the villagers.

"I'll check," said Zeus. But before he could fish his amulet from around his neck, a sound like the rumble of a hundred speeding chariots met the Olympians' ears.

They all turned toward the sound in surprise.

In the distance a great mound of earth had formed. Suddenly the mound exploded like a volcano.

The Olympians and villagers gasped. As they watched, a giant beanstalk pushed out of the crater where the mound had been. Quickly it sprouted up to the sky until it's tip-top disappeared into the clouds.

"Clamoring clams, that's one fast-growing plant!" Poseidon exclaimed.

Zeus grinned. "And you know what? I'm guessing it grew from a *Magic Seed*."

"Only one thing to do, right?" said Hades.

"Climb it!" they all cheered.

With their sights set on the distant beanstalk, the Olympians set off together on their next adventure.

ABOUT THE AUTHORS

Joan Holub has authored and/or illustrated over 140 children's books, including the *New York Times* bestselling picture book *Mighty Dads* (illustrated by James Dean) and *Little Red Writing* (illustrated by Melissa Sweet). She lives in North Carolina and at www.joanholub.com.

Suzanne Williams is the author of over fifty books for children, including the award-winning picture book *Library Lil* (illustrated by Steven Kellogg). She lives outside Seattle, Washington, and is online at www.suzanne-williams.com.

Together, Joan and Suzanne write the Goddess Girls, Heroes in Training, and Grimmtastic Girls series.

CHAPTER ONE

Surprise Attack!

Ouch!" ten-year-old Zeus yelled as a hot orange spark hit his shoulder.

"Sorry," said Hestia. "I'm trying to figure out how to control this thing."

She held up a long metal torch decorated with carvings. A bright flame danced in the shallow bowl at the top of the torch.

"Well, maybe you should try a little harder," Hera muttered under her breath.

Zeus knew that Hera was upset. Yesterday he and his five young Olympian friends had found the Olympic Torch and its eternal flame. Hera had hoped the magical object would be hers. But the magic only worked when Hestia held the torch.

Zeus tried changing the subject. "I think we'll get to that giant beanstalk in just a couple of hours."

He nodded into the distance. A tall green stalk with big leaves had sprouted up from the ground early that morning. The stalk had grown so tall that its top disappeared into the clouds. Pythia, the Oracle of Delphi, had sent them on a quest to find Magic Seeds, and the giant beanstalk looked like a good place to start.

Poseidon, whose eyes were the color of the ocean, rubbed his stomach. "If we find those

Magic Seeds, I just might eat them," he said. "We've been walking all morning, and we haven't eaten since last night."

"Hey! Is that a farmhouse?" said red-haired Demeter. She pointed into the distance. "Maybe we can get something to eat there."

Hera frowned. "Do we have to stop? We're not that far from the beanstalk now."

"Actually, I'm kind of hungry too," Hades admitted.

"It's not a bad idea to stop," Zeus reasoned. "We might need our strength to face . . . whatever's waiting for us at that stalk."

The other Olympians knew what he meant. Every time they went searching for a new magical object or a missing Olympian, they got into some kind of danger. Sometimes King Cronus of the Titans sent monsters to stop them. Or other Titans hurled fireballs at them, or tried to kidnap them, or worse.

Sure, the giant beanstalk looked like a harmless plant, but Zeus knew by now that anything could happen. And when it did, it would probably be bad.